Valegro

A Rising Star

The Blueberry Stories: Book Three

Carl Hester MBE FBHS with Janet Rising
with illustrations by Helena Öhmark

Matador
9 Priory Business Park,
Wistow Road, Kibworth Beauchamp,
Leicestershire. LE8 0RX
Tel: 0116 279 2299
Email: books@troubador.co.uk
Web: www.troubador.co.uk/matador
Twitter: @matadorbooks

ISBN 978 1788036 146

British Library Cataloguing in Publication Data.
A catalogue record for this book is available from the British Library.

Printed and bound in the UK by TJ International, Padstow, Cornwall
Typeset in 12pt Book Antiqua by Troubador Publishing Ltd, Leicester, UK

Matador is an imprint of Troubador Publishing Ltd

*This book is dedicated to all staff at Oakelbrook Mill,
past and present, who have played such an important
part in Blueberry's extraordinary rise to fame.*

Chapter One

"Steady now, Blueberry," whispered Carl, asking his mount to slow a fraction and listen to him. The little brown horse Blueberry, known in competitions by his registered name Valegro, was keen to do as his rider requested – but sometimes that meant he was too eager, and forgot to listen. A brilliant dressage horse has to have talent (which Blueberry had) and ability (which Blueberry possessed by the bucket-load), but he also has to listen to his rider and wait for the instructions to come, rather than do his own thing and hope his rider will catch up. Sometimes, Carl acknowledged, Blueberry was so keen to show him how well he understood the aids given by his rider's legs, hands and seat, his enthusiasm got the better of him and he anticipated what Carl wanted.

"You're one of the keenest equine pupils I've ever had," laughed Carl, again requesting that his mount shorten his stride and bring his legs higher under his body, taking shorter, but much more energetic, steps. This time Blueberry did as he was asked, arching his neck and feeling his energy go upward and be contained in his body, rather than move forward. As he did so Blueberry thought of The Silver Dancer, Carl's amazing metal statue of a dressage horse in piaffe, the most advanced, most elevated and graceful of all the dressage movements. Blueberry longed to dance like the sculpture, and as he sprang from one set of his diagonal legs to the other in his energetic trot he felt sure he resembled The Silver Dancer more than ever.

"Okay Blueberry," said Carl, loosening the reins and allowing his mount to stretch his neck and relax for a while in trot then walk, "that's enough for today. Good job!"

2

Dismounting, Carl handed the reins to Lydia, Blueberry's groom, who led him to the washing boxes where she unsaddled him and washed him down with warm water, drying him off under the glowing solarium lights.

Blueberry lifted his head and looked around at Brook Mill where he, and all the other dressage horses Carl trained, lived and worked. He always loved feeling the warm water on his back, running down his legs and cleaning the sweat from his coat. The crimson solarium lights made his muscles feel good – he had worked hard and now he enjoyed being pampered. With his shower and drying complete, Blueberry was led to his stable where a full net of hay awaited him.

As he tugged and chewed at his hay, Blueberry thought about his schooling session. He and the other horses at Brook Mill had only four schooling sessions scheduled every week, and Blueberry always looked forward to being ridden in either the indoor or outdoor arena. He particularly enjoyed being ridden by Carl – although the pupils and students also rode him. They were all good riders, and as Carl was always there to coach and encourage, inspire and direct, all the horses learned something at every session.

But with Carl in Blueberry's saddle, it was

different. With Carl, Blueberry thought, it was as though his rider spoke the same language as his horse, as though Carl knew exactly what Blueberry could do, even though Blueberry himself hadn't realised – until he did it with Carl. With some of the other riders, the little brown horse occasionally felt as though neither of them knew quite what was needed – possibly a little more leg from the rider here, a little less bend in the neck from Blueberry there. With Carl, it just flowed and it all seemed easy, effortless.

This was no accident; Carl made sure every lesson he conducted with his horses was progressive. He didn't ask any questions from his horses until he was certain they knew the answers – and he was certain they knew the answers because he had given them all the information in the lessons they had had before. That way, if he asked for half-pass, where the horse moved sideways and forward under his rider, he knew his horse's muscles had developed in previous schooling sessions, and the horse had learned to move away from the rider's leg and follow the opening given by the rider's rein – not to mention the feeling the rider gave the horse with his weight, and the direction indicated by the rider's own upper body. With Carl in his saddle, Blueberry felt as though he was a fully-trained dressage horse, with all the moves at the tips of his hooves.

Of course, all horses are capable of carrying out all the dressage movements you see in a dressage arena. They do them in the field, in play, on a chilly morning or when playing with other horses, but to carry out these movements under a rider and exactly when asked is more difficult. A bad rider can not only hamper a horse but actually block and prevent him from carrying out the movements. A good rider, on the other hand, can lead the horse into the movement and make the horse feel like he's flying! It was this feeling that Blueberry got whenever Carl rode him. The other pupils and students were good riders, and Blueberry could do the movements they asked for, but it was only with Carl that felt he had wings on his hooves. It was only with Carl that Blueberry felt he might just be like The Silver Dancer after all.

"How's the Badminton Young Dressage Horse of the Future today?" asked Lulu, the small, one-eyed, tan-coloured top-dog-of-the-yard, as she wriggled through the secret, Lulu-sized hole she had made at the back of Blueberry's stable and settled down on a pile of dropped hay next to her friend's front hooves.

Blueberry snorted and for a moment his

mind drifted back to the competition Lulu referred to, which he had won in the summer with Lucy in his saddle. At only four years old, he had beaten all the best four- and five-year old dressage horses in the country, including Uthopia, Carl's almost black stallion, a year older, and more experienced than Blueberry. It had been the most amazing day and Blueberry loved to remember it during his quiet moments, when all the grooms had finished their work for the day, and the yard at Brook Mill was dark and quiet. He loved revelling in his past achievements and dreaming of future glories came before sleep.

"Carl rode me today," Blueberry replied. "It felt really good – I'm beginning to understand how I need to keep my energy reserved in my quarters and when I get it right I feel as though my back is working as well as my legs, and my shoulders feel higher. When that happens, I can hardly hear my hoof beats on the arena's surface. It's as though I'm lighter and moving on air. It's very weird, but in a good way. I felt like The Silver Dancer!"

Lulu felt herself nodding. She had seen countless horses trained at Brook Mill. She liked nothing more than to sit with Carl while he taught his pupils – equine and human – and she hadn't wasted that time. She had soaked up all the information Carl imparted, she had watched the horses and understood what Carl was asking for, noticing the difference when a horse went well and when it didn't, realising what riders needed to do to improve themselves and their mounts. Lulu often thought her knowledge was somewhat wasted – she'd have made a great riding teacher, she thought, somewhat immodestly. If was a shame the humans didn't understand her.

"It's the young horses whose hooves make the most noise," she said. "The top dressage horses are almost silent they're so light on their feet. It's as though they hardly brush the surface of the arena."

Blueberry stopped chewing his hay for a moment while he digested this piece of information, storing it away in his brain to bring out and use later before turning his attention back to his hay. There wasn't much that could stop Blueberry eating – his appetite was legendary!

"When Carl rides me," Blueberry continued, grateful as always to have Lulu around as speaking his thoughts out loud helped him to make sense of them, "I feel as though I can be a brilliant dressage horse. I feel... well, it's as though Carl is not really riding me, more like he's *part* of me, like we're two beings fused together like... like..." Blueberry struggled to find the words.

"Like you're a centaur?" Lulu asked him, before realising her friend had no idea what a centaur was. "That's a mythical creature that is half-man, half-horse," she explained. She decided against telling Blueberry that the human part replaced the horse's head, she thought that might freak him out. No need to alarm him, she decided. After all, without a head, how would he eat?

"Exactly!" cried Blueberry, pausing in mid-chew. "That's just what it feels like. It's very weird, but rather wonderful at the same time."

Lulu lifted a hind leg and scratched behind one ear. Blueberry, she knew, was enjoying his lessons, loving his training and progressing fast. His dream was to be the best dressage horse in the world and if Lulu was any judge (and she *was*, she told herself), he was rushing towards reaching his true potential. If thinking about how he felt when he was learning his craft made the little brown horse pause from his food, Lulu acknowledged, he must surely be destined for the top!

Chapter Two

"Did you go to the big show?" asked Orange, the large chestnut horse with a white blaze and two white socks. He and Blueberry were turned out in the paddock behind the outdoor school, as they were every day. It was the end of summer; the leaves were thinking about turning to their autumn colours and drifting from the branches, the sun was

9

already travelling lower in the sky and birds were swooping and chirping before leaving for the warmer air and more abundant feeding grounds in the south.

"Oh I had the most amazing adventure," replied Blueberry, a little breathlessly but delighted his friend had asked because he so wanted to tell him all about it. He had enjoyed the most thrilling day of his life (so far, he thought, not wishing to close the door on other, possibly even more thrilling days in the future), and he was still buzzing from the excitement of it all.

"Go on then, tell me all about it," said Orange, recognising that Blueberry wanted to share without realising quite what he was in for.

"Well," began Blueberry, his eyes shining as he reassembled his thoughts to begin his account, not wanting to leave anything out, "Lydia woke me up early and plaited my mane, so I knew I was going to the big show with some of the other horses. It lasts for days, and we've seen the horsebox coming and going, so I was hoping I would be included. Then I had some breakfast and I could see Lydia loading the horsebox with all my tack and I couldn't wait to follow it up the ramp…"

"Er, any chance you could skip to the more interesting part?" asked Orange, realising he

10

was in for a long story. He hoped his comment wouldn't upset Blueberry – he was his best friend and he knew he was only excited and wanted to share that excitement.

"What? Oh, yes, okay," said Blueberry, his mind scrolling forward. "Lydia didn't come with me, Lucy did, so I was looking forward to her riding me. After a bit of a journey in the horsebox with Uti and some of the other horses, we arrived at a competition."

At the mention of a competition, Orange shuddered. Although the big chestnut horse loved learning his lessons at Brook Mill, and wanted nothing more than to become a dressage horse, he was less than keen on competing. Being of nervous disposition Orange, gained confidence in areas he was familiar with and disliked being taken out of his comfort zone. Unfortunately, any competition was very definitely outside that zone, which meant that Orange found it impossible to concentrate on what he had learned when he was anywhere but home. This, as you might expect, was a major setback in his career, although Carl still had hopes that the big chestnut horse would grow more comfortable with experience. Sadly, Orange didn't share his confidence.

"It was a very big and busy showground," continued Blueberry, pretending not to notice

Orange's shudder. "There were so many horses, horseboxes and people. Anyway, after a while Carl mounted Uti and they went off to warm up for their test…"

"How did he do?" asked Orange, politely.

Blueberry told him he had done very well before continuing with his own story. "Where was I?" he asked, staring into the distance.

"Uti went off to do his test…" said Orange, helpfully.

"Oh yes, so I had to wait, and wait and wait. It seemed that my test was much later in the day so there was quite a lot of hanging around. So, I chatted with Lulu for a bit – she had sneaked into the cab of the horsebox when no-one was looking so she had managed to come along, too – and had a spot of lunch, some rather nice hay, and looked around at the other horses warming up. As usual, they all seemed much bi…, er… I mean they all seemed very polished and professional," said Blueberry, seemingly distracted. He had almost admitted that the other horses were all much bigger than he was.

His mind wandered back to the great day the previous summer when he had won the Badminton Young Dressage Horse of the Future with Lucy riding him. The other horses at the competition had all looked down their noses and mistaken him for an entrant in the Pony

12

Club competition because he had been so much smaller than they were. And Blueberry had felt small, because they made him feel small. It wasn't until he was in the dressage arena that he decided to show them what he was made of. He had been so determined that his dressage test had made a brilliant impression on the judge, who awarded him first place. He, Blueberry, the horse the other horses had said was too small, had won the title and shown them all! Even so, he was still sensitive about his lack of height, and didn't feel inclined to share his worry with Orange. Blueberry hoped that if he didn't mention it, and he didn't think about it, his insecurities about his height might go away.

"So the other horses were stiff competition," continued Blueberry, putting his negative thoughts behind him. "Lulu, of course, was very encouraging, and helped me control my nerves because the longer I had to wait for my class, the worse they seemed to get. Before, I couldn't wait to get into the arena and show off what I'd learned but the waiting this time made me feel quite jittery. I wished I could have done my test early in the day because that would have been better. It's funny, isn't it, I thought I would be confident after my big win last season, but it made the pressure worse somehow. I expected to do well this time, and that made me anxious."

Orange nodded. He knew his nerves would have been in shreds and he was sure what Blueberry thought of as nerves were tiny compared to his own.

"So, I talked to Lulu about it, and she had a really good idea which worked a treat – you might like to try it," said Blueberry.

"Any ideas gratefully received," said Orange.

"Lulu suggested I tell myself that the nerves I was feeling were excitement. That instead of being nervous, I was *excited* about the test to come. So I tried it, and it worked! I found myself looking forward to demonstrating what I've learned. The more I thought about being excited, the more I wanted to get in to the arena and show everyone!"

Orange looked doubtful. Lulu's advice had obviously helped Blueberry – but Orange knew that Blueberry loved showing off his training, and what he had thought of as nerves were probably excitement and impatience anyway. Orange decided he would try out Lulu's idea but he had little confidence in it which, in itself, he acknowledged, might be enough to stop it working for him. You had to believe in these things, he thought.

"So, Lucy tacked me up and got me all ready but she was still in her normal clothes and I knew she'd have to change into her posh

14

riding gear," continued Blueberry. "I thought, she's cutting it a bit fine, because if my tack is on then I'll need to be warming up in a minute or two, but still she didn't get changed. I began to worry that if she didn't smarten herself up soon, I wouldn't be able to compete. All that excitement for nothing! But then – oh Orange, this is the best bit, you'll never guess…"

"Ummm… Carl rode you?" suggested Orange.

"YES!" cried Blueberry, slightly miffed that Orange had guessed his big reveal. He had been looking forward to seeing his friend's reaction when he told him, and had imagined Orange saying, *Ooo, you're joking! Really? Carl? Wow, that's amazing!* But Orange had guessed. The surprise was ruined. Blueberry decided not to dwell on it.

"Yes, Carl rode me! Isn't that something? I could hardly believe it when Lucy legged him up into my saddle and we headed off to warm up. I couldn't help thinking that Carl might just be warming me up for Lucy, and that she might arrive at any moment in her black jacket and shiny boots and swap places. But she didn't!"

"So what happened then?" asked Orange, fully interested in Blueberry's story now it was getting to the climax – his actual dressage test.

"The competition was big, lots of horses

entered. There were crowds of people watching too, and the arena was surrounded by posters and banners, and there were other arenas I could see, with horses performing their tests. It was all very distracting with horses being ridden around, people rushing about and loudspeakers barking out results – it was a very large show. Are you all right?"

Orange nodded unconvincingly. It sounded terrible and he gulped. He was so grateful not to have been taken along.

"I was so excited, Carl had to ride me around for a long time before I would settle but eventually I did. When we entered the arena I felt Carl's hand on my neck to reassure me, and I felt that everything was going to be fine. I just had to do my best. So I did and it was quite easy to do that because Carl was riding me and I felt I could do anything! It all seemed to pass very quickly, and when Carl rode me out of the arena on a long rein I couldn't help feeling very proud – although I wonder whether I could have improved one or two transitions. Uti says there is always something you know you could have improved on, and wish you had a second chance to show the judges. I couldn't see them, the judges I mean, they must have been in the sheds – like Lulu told me they would be – and I made sure I didn't try to look for them. They

16

don't like that, apparently. They prefer to think you don't know they're there, and that they're hidden. I think Carl knows they're in the sheds. Do you think Carl knows?"

"I would say that if Lulu knows the judges are in the sheds then Carl certainly knows it," said Orange, firmly.

"Yes, of course you're right," agreed Blueberry.

"Well it sounds like you had a great day," said Orange, looking sideways at the juicy green grass by the hedge. It was about time, he thought, that they both got back to the serious business of grazing.

"But that's not the best bit!" cried Blueberry who, uncharacteristically, had put thoughts of grazing on hold, his day out had been such an experience. "I haven't told you the rest!"

"Oh, my apologies, do go on," said Orange, making a brilliant job of not sounding disappointed and hoping his friend couldn't hear his stomach rumbling.

"Because it was some time after my test when Lulu came galloping back from looking at the scoreboard with Carl to tell me I had done pretty well, and that I had to go back into the arena for the presentation."

"What scoreboard?" asked Orange, interested.

17

"Apparently, all the horses' test scores are put up on a scoreboard for everyone to see," explained Blueberry.

"Everyone can see them?"

"Yes, even the spectators. Absolutely *everyone* can see the score the judges gave you."

"How awful!" cried Orange. "Imagine the humiliation if you've done badly."

"Yes," agreed Blueberry, "although Lulu said that nobody is too worried about that because everyone understands how anyone can have an off-day, and you should be more interested in improving your scores as you progress, rather than getting the *best* score. It's more about what the judge writes about you on your score sheet than the actual score itself, because there will always be good things in a test, and other parts which need working on. And, of course, Lulu says that horses are not machines and everyone understands that."

"Oh, I see," said Orange, not really seeing. "So what was your score?"

"I'm coming to that bit," said Blueberry. "So Lucy legged up Carl again and we made our way back to the arena and the voice on the loudspeaker started saying who had won..."

"So where did you come?" interrupted Orange.

"First!" cried Blueberry, thinking he would

burst with pride. "I won! It was awesome, Orange, just amazing. The competition was sponsored by something called Shearwater…"

"They what?" asked Orange.

"Er, Lulu said companies sponsor competitions, I don't understand it much myself, to be honest."

"Okay," said Orange, not so interested in sponsorship that he felt the need to understand how it worked.

"Carl rode me into the arena and someone presented me with some huge rosettes and a sash to wear around my neck, as well as a lovely dark blue rug with *Shearwater Dressage Horse* written on it, so everyone knew I'm a dressage horse. Then I had to stand still while people took something called a photograph and everyone clapped, which was amazing. Finally, Carl and I galloped around the arena in a lap on honour, which was great fun!" Blueberry said, proudly.

"Congratulations!" said Orange, warmly. He was thrilled for his friend – mainly because he could see it meant so much to him. Not just the win, but that fact that he had won with Carl.

Blueberry sighed. It had been such a fantastic day, a day of dreams fulfilled. He thought he would never forget how he had felt when he knew he had won, how his heart seemed to swell with pride and he heard the people clapping and cheering as he cantered around the arena with his ribbons fluttering in the breeze, his prize rug on his back, his white-bandaged legs lifting higher and higher with sheer joy.

"Wow, you certainly did have an adventure," said Orange. "You're on your way to the big time, Blueberry," he continued, glad for his friend. "It sounds as though your dreams really are coming true."

"Yes," sighed Blueberry, suddenly hungry. "Let's eat!"

Chapter Three

It was about a week after Blueberry's wonderful success with Carl in the Shearwater Four-Year-Old Championship that Clyde, the light-ginger coloured cat, went missing. Lydia remembered seeing him the day before, when he had graciously accepted some chicken she had offered him from her sandwiches, and Carl said he had seen Clyde's marmalade tail twitching from the underside of a bush outside the yard the previous afternoon, but no-one could remember seeing him at all since then.

Lydia was worried. She loved both Clyde and Bonnie, his tortoiseshell-and-white sister, and when evening stables had been completed, the horses all given their last haynets and final feeds of the day, checked over, their beds tidied and skipped out and the tack room locked for the night, only Bonnie could be seen tucking into her bowl of cat nibbles next to her water bowl. The cats' dinners were placed on top of one of the two circular brick containers in the yard which surrounded the ornamental trees, so that the dogs knew it wasn't for them and left them alone. At least that was the theory; Willow could often be seen with his head high, sniffing the bowls, wondering whether he could steal the food, or whether he dared to surprise one (or both) of the cats while they were eating and enjoy a chase around the yard. But in his heart the big mastiff-cross, who had come from a canine rescue centre to live at Brook Mill, knew that Carl would be furious if he so much as licked the cats' food, or, even worse, chased the cats themselves. Willow was well aware that chasing anything at Brook Mill was strictly forbidden. With only Bonnie eating and no sign

22

of Clyde anywhere, Lydia's worry grew into anxiety and she tried very hard not to panic. Where was Clyde? What could have happened to him?

In her mind Lydia imagined all sorts of terrible things. After checking under the shrub where Carl had spotted Clyde's tail (no sign of Clyde) she walked all around the yard, the outside arena, the indoor arena, the car park and the outside stables, calling the cat's name, but there was still no sign of the ginger puss. With her heart in her mouth, and hoping she *wouldn't* find Clyde at her next search area, Lydia walked down the drive, through the big electric gates and out to the lane where the cars hurtled along with no consideration to wandering cats or wildlife. Still no sign of Clyde – thank goodness, thought Lydia. She had been terrified she might find Clyde hurt, or worse, by the side of the road. But no, no lost ginger cat there. It was getting dark and although Lydia knew that wouldn't bother Clyde, being able to see better in the gloom than any human due to the clever design nature had evolved for his eyes, it meant Lydia's search would have to wait until the morning.

"Where are you?" Lydia whispered to the wind, hoping somehow a message of her concern might reach the missing cat and bring him back to her.

"You know what cats are like," one of the other grooms said. "They're always wandering off. Clyde will be back when he gets hungry, don't you worry!"

But Clyde had never wandered off before. He and Bonnie had come to live at Brook Mill when they were kittens, and neither of them had gone missing before. Lydia wasn't comforted and she slept badly, waking in the night to lie in her bed above the stable yard and worry about Clyde.

"Wherever do you think Clyde might have gone?" Blueberry asked Lulu.

The little tan-coloured dog tore her nose away from a particularly enticing scent and looked up at him, puzzled. "Clyde?" she said. "Oh, *Clyde*, that cat person, the orangey-coloured one, you mean? Is he not about?"

Blueberry knew that Lulu had a very low opinion of the cats. She said they didn't do anything and that they were not worth spending any time on. Blueberry had decided to research the cats himself, however, and had found Clyde a lot nicer to talk to than Lulu had suggested. Blueberry had decided that he liked the cats. What he didn't want, however, was to upset his one-eyed friend. After all, Lulu had helped him more than anyone (except Carl) at Brook Mill, and he would have hated for her to think he didn't respect her opinion.

"Clyde hasn't come back for dinner and Lydia's really upset," Blueberry explained, deciding to make it all about Lydia, who he knew Lulu adored. It wouldn't do for her to think that he, Blueberry, was worried about Clyde.

"Oh no, poor Lydia," agreed Lulu.

Blueberry was just congratulating himself, thinking his plan had worked and he had successfully worked the conversation around to Lydia, steering Lulu away from another moan about cats, when he was proved wrong.

"That's just so typical of cats," the little dog continued, crossly, "they've no consideration for anyone but themselves. It's all me, me, me, with cats. Or mew, mew, mew!" Lulu snorted in laugher, pleased with her joke. Blueberry pretended to laugh with her, but he too was worried for Clyde. Where could the little cat be?

"He's probably shut in someone's shed, or he's more likely to just be hunting. Cats," Lulu continued, rather testily, "are allowed to chase things. I've always noticed that nobody tells cats off for chasing things. Oh no. But if Willow so much as sniffs towards the guinea fowl, Carl is on to him like lightning. It's one rule for dogs and quite another for cats!"

Blueberry decided that the no-chasing rule for dogs might just be why Lulu was so against the cats. She liked to think she could do whatever she liked at Brook Mill, being top dog and all, but clearly, she had a bee in her bonnet about the whole *cats-can* and *dogs-can't* scenario. Blueberry had heard Lydia tell someone that one of the horses had a bee in their bonnet about something and he hadn't really understood what she had meant. The horse clearly wore no bonnet, and there were no bees about, but Blueberry decided it was just a figure of speech and didn't actually involve bonnets or bees. Sometimes, the little brown horse thought, what people said made no sense. Now he used the same figure of speech about Lulu, he understood it more.

"Anyway," said Blueberry, "Clyde isn't here and Lydia is concerned so I hope he returns tomorrow so she will be happy again. Don't you?"

"Of course," said Lulu. "Absolutely. No doubt about it. For Lydia's sake I hope the cat's back as soon as."

Blueberry almost believed her.

Clyde didn't return the next day, or the day after that. Everyone on the yard was instructed to turn the place upside down to check he hadn't become trapped anywhere. The tack room was given a thorough going-through ("Good excuse for a clear-out," said Carl), the horsebox was inspected inside, outside and even under the

26

bonnet when someone remembered reading about a cat climbing into a car engine and travelling over eighty miles without the driver knowing anything about it. The hay barn was sorted through with the aid of torches. The fields were inspected. Carl even searched his own house, even though the cats never went in there. Everyone was instructed to check their own cars, and the feed room was turned inside out but without success. Clyde remained on the missing list.

When Blueberry and Orange went hacking that afternoon their riders, Lydia and Angela, kept a look-out for any sight of ginger fur, and called Clyde's name at regular intervals. But there was still no sign of the missing feline. It was as though he had vanished from the face of the earth – or from Brook Mill and the surrounding area, anyway.

"I can't help thinking something terrible has happened to him," wailed Lydia as she dismounted from Blueberry in the yard. "It's just not like him to stray."

Blueberry nuzzled his friend's arm. He hated to see her in such distress and wished with all his heart he could help – but he could no more find Clyde than anyone else. The cat had disappeared and no amount of wishing would bring him back.

Chapter Four

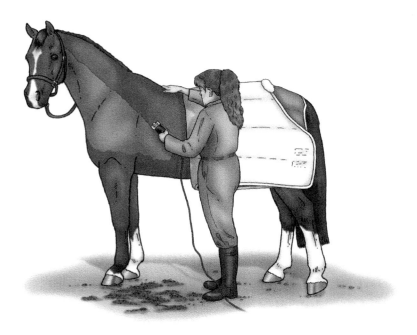

Autumn brought with it the beautiful show of red and gold as the trees shut down for the winter, shedding their leaves which piled up around the yard and caused much sighing amongst the grooms. No sooner had they swept up and made the place look immaculate, when more leaves drifted down. It was as though the trees were laughing at them, daring them to pick up every leaf as it fell. Blueberry liked watching the leaves change colour. They reminded him of The Silver Dancer, the metal sculpture of the dancing horse in front of Carl's house on which colour-changing lights in green, amber and red were trained, causing the horse to glow and flicker as though moving. From his corner stable, Blueberry never tired of watching The Silver Dancer through the stable archway. With the leaves echoing his inspiration, Blueberry enjoyed watching them release from their branches and float down, before landing crisply on the yard and bouncing along to the corners as though they too could dance.

Orange wasn't so keen on autumn. "Everything is dying," he moaned. "It's depressing. The days are shorter, the nights are longer, the air is cold and damp. I can't wait for the summer to return."

Blueberry disagreed. He enjoyed the changing seasons. True, he would have preferred longer days – all the better for spending time in the field grazing – but his stable was warm and cosy and he could enjoy watching his breath escape from his nostrils and billow into the yard like temporary clouds. He liked to take a deep breath and see how much he could expel. The overhang above his stable meant he could look out when it rained and see what was going on without getting wet, and it seemed to him that the trees weren't dying, but going to sleep until the warmth of the spring would wake them up again. Blueberry had seen four autumns come and go so he knew it wouldn't go on forever. Besides, now he was competing he knew there would be competitions to go to, which would make the autumn and winter months seem to pass faster.

Lulu shared Orange's thoughts regarding the changing season. "This damp isn't good for my bones," she told Blueberry one day, when the rain fell in a persistent drizzle which soaked everyone and made Lulu's paws wet. Blueberry's schooling session had taken place in the indoor school, but, with one whole long side open above the boards, the damp seeped in, making it seem even colder inside than it was in the open air.

Blueberry didn't understand why the damp was bad for Lulu's bones. He knew she liked to chew on a bone or two – he'd seen her growling at Willow when the big dog had finished his own bone and had dared to ask whether she'd consider sharing hers. Blueberry guessed Lulu's not-at-all-polite growl meant the answer was no. Lulu shared her wisdom with him, she shared her thoughts but it seemed that sharing her bone with Willow was a share too far.

Even the changing weather didn't stop Lulu being with Carl during the schooling sessions. She would jump up onto a chair onto which a rug had been thrown, circle a few times to make sure she was comfortable and facing the right way, before sinking down, placing her head on her paws and keeping her one eye on proceedings. She hated to miss anything.

Blueberry worked hard during his schooling sessions, paying strict attention to his riders and working out what they wanted him to do. Carl rode him regularly – but most of the time he was ridden by the pupils and students. Although they were all accomplished riders, they were all different and their experience varied. Some of the pupils were still finding their own confidence in their ability and Blueberry could sometimes feel hesitation in their aids. They were not totally certain what they wanted him to do, and this in turn made him doubt his own ability. His ears twitched, his chin wobbled, and he found himself thinking more about what the rider might or might not want, instead of giving his all to carrying out the movements asked for. It was very strange and very different to when Carl rode him. When Carl rode him, Blueberry felt he could do anything!

31

With the better riders, Blueberry felt their confidence in their hands, their seat, their legs – their whole attitude – as they asked him to go forward, to slow down, to move sideways. These riders made their horses' confidence soar, enabling them to move with a fluency they hadn't known they possessed. With these riders in his saddle Blueberry found he didn't just carry out whatever Carl instructed them to do, he carried it out with flair so that Carl nodded his approval. With these riders, Blueberry found that he could lift his legs higher, his back became supple, he moved with ease and grace. It was almost like being ridden by Carl – but not quite. There was still a tiny piece of the jigsaw missing which was miraculously found whenever Carl sat in his saddle.

Even in the indoor school the leaves blew in like confetti, which made Orange snort and Bonnie the cat chase them as though they were mice, and if the wind was in the wrong direction the rain blew in too, making Blueberry blink as he trotted past the long, open side, his forelock hanging in wet tendrils on his face.

Blueberry particularly enjoyed hacking out at this time of year. The flies, which pestered the horses during the summer months, no matter how much fly repellent was applied, had disappeared and the fallen leaves made a crisp, crunching sound as the horses walked through them, leaving the woods more open and light, the bare trees extending their branches upwards like hands reaching for the sky. Blueberry watched the squirrels burying acorns for winter, and it was at this time of year that he was more likely to catch a glimpse of wild deer. With winter promising to follow autumn, Blueberry noticed his coat growing longer. When the sun shone brightly and the day was warm, the little brown horse felt sweat on his neck and between his hind legs, proving that he was working correctly from his engine in his hindquarters. It was during these late autumn months when Blueberry noticed the horses at Brook Mill getting a makeover.

"What's happened to you?" Blueberry asked Orange. The chestnut horse looked somehow different. His coat seemed lighter than the deep chestnut colour he was used to seeing. His winter coat seemed somehow smoother, his legs looked thinner.

"Oh don't ask!" replied Orange, his ears twitching back and forth in distress. "I've been clipped!"

"Oh," said Blueberry, remembering how some of the other horses had been clipped the previous year. He had seen them being led out of their stables and then return, a while later, with their coats shaved off. He had thought it a strange thing to do when the weather was turning colder and a horse was in need of his own designer coat, but the horses all had duvet-type rugs on to keep them warm, and they hadn't seemed at all bothered.

"Are you warm enough?" asked Blueberry.

"Oh yes, this rug is lovely and cosy," Orange replied. "I just feel a bit... well... sort of ... light and a bit naked, if you know what I mean. It's strange. I expect I'll get used to it."

"Did it hurt?" Blueberry asked.

"No. But it did tickle and the noise was worrying. Lydia made sure I was okay with it before she started, though, very patient she was. Whatever next, eh?"

Blueberry didn't know the answer to that. He noticed that it was only the older horses, the ones who were working and competing which were clipped, so he hoped he would be too. When he next saw Lulu, who was passing by on her way to check out a car which had driven in and parked up at the far end of the outdoor school, he asked her about being clipped.

"Ahhh, yes, it's that time of year," said Lulu, nodding. "I expect you'll get the treatment any day now."

"But why do it now?" asked Blueberry. "It's chilly, I need my coat."

"Been sweating have you, kiddo?" asked Lulu. "Worked up a sweat while you've been schooling, or even out hacking?"

Blueberry thought hard, "Well yes, I have."

"So you've answered your own question, haven't you," said Lulu.

Blueberry's chin twitched. It tended to wobble about when he was worried about something, or didn't understand what Lulu was telling him.

"If you weren't clipped, and you kept your long coat and sweated every time you had to work hard – because dressage is quite hard work, isn't it…?" Lulu began.

Blueberry agreed. Dressage may look as though the horse is just walking, trotting and cantering around but when it is done well it is very strenuous. It is, as Lulu had often told Blueberry, the equivalent of a human performing a mixture of gymnastics and ballet. And nobody, Lulu had told him, thought gymnastics and ballet were easy to do.

"… so, if you had to work hard while wearing your own long coat," continued Lulu, "it would be very difficult, you wouldn't enjoy it and you would lose condition. Do you agree?"

Blueberry did. He didn't like the sound of it. Nobody, as far as he knew, performed gymnastics or ballet in a fur coat.

"So, there's your answer, kiddo," finished Lulu, hurrying out of the yard to investigate the parked car – which turned out to be someone who had come to mend a broken automatic drinker in a stable, rather than someone up to no good, which was what Lulu was afraid of. People *who were up to no good* were always on Lulu's hit-list. She hadn't found one yet, but Lulu was certain it was only a matter of time. She had to be on her toes. Drop your guard, Lulu believed, and that was when people *who were up to no good* were bound to strike.

The very next day, Blueberry was led out of his stable and taken to the washing area. The whirling sound of a small machine reached his ears, which he swivelled around to hear. The noise was coming from a small machine Lydia held in her hand. Blueberry was going to get a hair cut!

Blueberry bent his neck to look at the machine. Knowing how nosy her charge was, Lydia let him sniff it, talking soothingly to him the whole time.

"These are clippers, Blueberry," she told him. "They won't hurt you but they might tickle a bit. Shall we see what they can do?"

Even though he trusted Lydia, Blueberry still braced himself as she laid the blades of the clippers on his shoulder. He felt the vibration through his skin. Lydia was right, it didn't hurt. Orange was right, too, it did tickle a bit. He relaxed. Lydia started clipping against the lay of the coat and whirls of soft, dark brown, Blueberry hair floated down to the floor. Soon, Blueberry was surrounded by bits that used to be part of him, and his once long coat on his neck, shoulder and body was transformed into a close covering as soft as suede.

"You're a nice colour," remarked Lydia. "You never know what you're going to get when you clip horses – they can be a totally different colour underneath their winter coat. I've known some chestnuts turn out pencil-lead grey. You're a lighter shade than your top coat, a blueberry-grey colour. No nasty surprises there!"

Blueberry stood still, feeling weird. The clippers felt strange as they travelled over his body. He felt a draught as his coat fell to the floor and Lydia threw a rug over his quarters once she had clipped most of his back – she left a patch in the centre in a saddle shape where his saddle would go so that the short, clipped coat wouldn't feel prickly when he wore it. After a while the little horse tugged at his haynet and thought little of his makeover – until it was time to clip his belly. One of the other grooms held up one of his fore legs to keep him still and stretch the skin underneath so that Lydia, bending down, could clip off the hair smoothly and quickly. The further back towards his hind legs Lydia went, the more the clippers tickled, and Blueberry felt his skin shudder – just as it did when he shook off a fly.

"Oh Blueberry, try to keep still," wailed Lydia. "It's like trying to clip corrugated cardboard when you do that!"

Blueberry tried, but it was very difficult. It wasn't as though he was shuddering on purpose, it was a totally involuntary reflex. Lydia managed to finish, but then she had his stifle to tackle and with the hair growing in all directions, it wasn't easy. But Lydia had clipped hundreds of horses and she made quick work of the site. All the time she checked the tension in the clippers, checked that the blades were still sharp and not getting too hot. With all the friction of clipping, blades can heat up and cause a good horse to fidget. No horse enjoys being clipped with hot blades!

Then it was time to clip the legs, which was not easy. Dressage horses need a clean, crisp outline. Fluffy, toy pony legs, will not do! Finally, Lydia very gently clipped around Blueberry's face. It was a difficult and delicate job, but it was swiftly finished – even his ears, which had to be bent over in order for the hair to be clipped off against the lay of the coat.

Finally, a fully made-over Blueberry was wiped over with a cloth to remove any remaining hairs and Lydia stood back to inspect her work. No tufts anywhere. No missed bits of coat. No hairy heels or snipped off pieces of mane and, most importantly, no lines visible so you could tell where the clippers had travelled. A well-clipped horse looks a picture and you can't see any lines. A badly-clipped horse, Lulu had told Blueberry, looks as though it has been clipped with a knife and fork. Bad clipping wasn't tolerated at Brook Mill!

"Not bad!" Lydia said, pleased with her work. Blueberry, meanwhile, hadn't been idle – he'd polished off a whole haynet and was looking around for more. With a new, heavier quilted rug over his clipped coat, Blueberry was led back to his stable where he looked out over his door to show off his new, streamlined head and neck. He had, he acknowledged, been looking a bit tatty lately, with his fluffy winter coat. Now he felt sleek and streamlined, ready for anything. He couldn't wait to show off his new look to Lulu.

Chapter Five

The days turned colder as the days shortened. One week, over several nights, the sound of loud bangs reached the stable yard. Blueberry looked out over his stable door to see explosions in the sky. The darkness was lit up by different coloured lights – accompanied by loud bangs and cracks – and then they just disappeared. Blueberry liked looking at the lights, but Orange

40

backed into his stable and hid his head in the corner, wishing it would all go away.

"They're not coming any closer, I think it's quite safe," Blueberry told him.

But Orange didn't agree. "It's aliens," he said, "visitors from outer space. I've heard about them. It can't be good; it can only be bad."

Blueberry wasn't convinced, knowing that Orange always thought the worst. He continued to watch the loud lights, fascinated by the randomness of them. He saw them erupt over the clock tower. Then they burst momentarily over the left roof, and then the right roof. They were all over the place and it was impossible to anticipate where they would appear next, even though Blueberry tried to guess. He got it right a few times, but not very often. After a few hours they stopped and after a few more days there were no more bangs and lights at all. If it had been aliens, Blueberry told Orange, it seemed they had got bored and had gone away.

One damp day, after morning stables when the yard had been made spick and span, Blueberry noticed a number of cars creeping along the drive and past the yard to the car park.

"What's going on?" he asked Orange. Orange didn't know, but he said he hoped it wasn't going to involve him in any way.

Soon, people began to drift into the yard,

and were directed by a woman Blueberry didn't know, to the indoor school. The woman knew Carl – he and she had chatted for a while beforehand, and the woman kept writing things on her clipboard whenever she spoke to any of the visitors. By this time, all the horses were looking out over their stable doors, curious about their break in routine. The grooms tacked up Dolendo, Orange and Blueberry, tying them up in their stables so they couldn't break their tack or rub their bits on the doors. Blueberry could hear Orange next door, his lower lip smacking against his upper lip, which he did whenever he was anxious. Blueberry was excited – whatever was going on, he was going to be included. He didn't want to be left out!

Dolendo, a big leggy chestnut with a wide blaze that Blueberry didn't know very well as he was working at a higher level, was led out first and Blueberry could see him warming up in the outdoor school with one of the students on board. Maybe, he thought, they were having a competition, a dressage test in the indoor school, and all those people were going to judge them. He wondered whether he would be able to hear what they had to say. Blueberry couldn't wait to see what was going to happen. He looked forward to showing off his new, sleek, clipped look to everyone.

After a while another of the students came to fetch Blueberry, leading him into the outdoor school and mounting. Blueberry knew Dolendo was in the indoor school (he could just see his head as he trotted past the long open side) and he could hear Carl talking. It was just as though Dolendo was being schooled as usual. But all those people, whose cars Blueberry could see in the car park, had to be in there watching.

It was a chilly day and Blueberry felt his back go up as he and his rider, a girl called Emily who often rode him, steered him around the school. Clipped, his rug stripped off and suddenly outside in the open air made Blueberry shiver. He hunched himself up against the cold, his back high, wanting to buck and play to get warm. He knew, however, that such a display of bad manners was not befitting a top dressage horse so he obeyed Emily, trotting around and warming his muscles. Emily kept him going forward, keeping her aids light, unwilling to give him any excuse to misbehave. Until Blueberry was warm, and she felt his back lower to its usual place, Emily wasn't taking any chances!

Warmed up and moving freely, Blueberry and Emily finally entered the indoor school where Carl stood. As he walked in further, however, Blueberry was surprised to see a semi-circle of people sitting on chairs with their backs to the walls of the arena, some with rugs over their knees, listening to what Carl was saying. It was very strange, thought Blueberry.

Blueberry caught sight of Willow, walking along the semi-circle, accepting pats and rubs from the audience. Then he spotted Lulu, curled up on one of the spectator's laps, looking a bit smug at finding herself a nice, warm place to sit.

Blueberry walked around the school, half his attention on Emily and half his attention on Carl and the audience watching him. He heard his name – Carl was telling them all about him, his history and his stage of training. His heart swelled with pride when he heard him say he rated him for the future, and that he was a horse to watch. Did Carl really think that? For a few moments Blueberry was lost in a daydream – a wonderful daydream where he and Carl were the best dressage combination in the whole world. He imagined the people watching him now telling their friends in the future, 'Yes, I saw Blueberry – I mean Valegro – when he was just a four-year-old. He looked very smart clipped out.'

"So, this walk you see Blueberry doing here, this at the moment is probably only a seven or eight walk," Carl said, bringing Blueberry back to earth with a thud.

What did Carl mean, thought Blueberry,

44

his was only a seven or eight walk? Was that good? It didn't sound like it could be very good if Carl described it as ONLY a seven or eight walk.

"You can see that the hind feet overlap the tracks made by the front feet, but not by as much as the previous horse. The last horse you saw had a nine or ten walk, you remember." Carl continued, "It's fine to have only a seven or eight walk at this stage of a young horse's training as it will make collection easier for Blueberry in this pace. This in turn will make it easier for him to learn piaffe and passage, the very advanced movements required in Grand Prix tests later in his career."

Blueberry felt his chin wobble. Dolendo had a nine or ten walk, which had to be much better than a seven or eight walk. He had to improve that. He forgot that Dolendo was a whole year older than he, that he had a whole year's worth of schooling in front of Blueberry.

"But when you see this horse in his best pace," Carl was saying to his attentive audience, as Emily asked Blueberry to canter around the school and the little brown horse leapt into his amazing, ground-covering and bouncy stride, "you can see that his canter is easily a nine or ten canter."

Blueberry heard a murmur rumble through

45

the spectators. The quality of his canter wasn't lost on this audience.

"Some people have suggested that this horse will have trouble collecting in canter because his canter is so huge," Carl went on as Blueberry continued at his impressive pace, "but I don't believe that. He's working well and, mark my words, he's one to watch, this horse. We're all very excited about him."

Blueberry hardly heard much more. His mind was buzzing with thoughts about his walk, he *had* to get it up to a nine or ten walk, he decided. And it seemed he had another worry along the same lines – that of his canter collection. Wasn't that what he was working on now in his lessons? Wasn't that when his riders asked him to go slower, but with the same energy – and sometimes more energy – as when he went faster? So it seemed he needed to think about his canter, and try to get the same energy he had in that pace in all his paces, even when he was collected and travelling slower.

There was only one way for his energy to go if he slowed down, thought Blueberry. If it couldn't go forward it would have to go somewhere, so maybe the only way was upward. Upward – yes, thought the little brown horse, his chin wobbling with all his hard thinking – that was collection. He needed to

46

keep some of the energy inside him, rather than letting it go forward in speed. His energy wasn't all used up, it was... *contained*. It was *collected*. He collected his energy and waited to release it in whichever direction, at whichever pace, his rider asked. Forward, sideways, backward, and even upward-and-forward combined in passage and piaffe. Blueberry felt much more certain about his schooling having worked out about collection in his own mind. Now he had to work to put it into practice.

After a few more minutes, Emily asked Blueberry to leave the indoor school and Orange walked in, his eyes rolling as he tried to look at all the people. He did hope this wasn't a competition. He so hated being looked at and judged by everyone – it was too much pressure.

Emily led Blueberry back to his stable, untacked him, rugged him up and gave him a sugar lump.

"Well done, Blueberry," she whispered to him, patting his neck. "You were very good."

A full haynet hung in the corner but Blueberry, uncharacteristically, stood thinking rather than eating. He had just been ridden around while Carl talked, so he knew he hadn't been in a test or competition but he still had plenty to think about. He would work to collect his walk. He remembered something Lulu had told him about how Carl said that walk was the one pace that couldn't be changed. Even so, Blueberry was determined to do just that!

He had to prove wrong whoever had said he would find collection in canter difficult. It wasn't enough just to be schooled every day, Blueberry decided, he had to try harder. He had to work to achieve his goal, to be the best dressage horse in the world because, clearly, it wasn't going to be easy. Blueberry vowed to do what Carl was always saying – to *make it happen*. He was so engrossed in his thoughts, he didn't even hear Orange return.

Suddenly, everyone who had been watching in the indoor school arrived in the yard. They wandered around, patting the horses and asking Carl questions. Blueberry received his fair share of visitors, and he was only too happy to chat. People took photographs, patted Willow and Lulu who had accompanied them in the manner of party hosts, marvelled at the guinea fowl huddled in a corner of the field, and went to admire The Silver Dancer, piaffing, as always, on the lawn. It was quite a party but eventually it broke up. People drifted away, calling their thanks. Cars trundled past the yard on their way out and Brook Mill became quiet again, the grooms turning out some horses in the fields, and giving other horses lunch.

"What was that?" Blueberry managed to ask Lulu before she dashed off to Carl's for a snack.

"A demo," said Lulu. "It's short for *demonstration*. Carl gives them now and again for dressage enthusiasts. They come and absorb all he can tell them in the two to three hours of watching his horses. They love it. Did you enjoy it?"

"Yes," said Blueberry, "I did. And I learnt something, too." He explained to Lulu his thoughts on collection and Lulu looked up at him and panted her thoughts.

"Spot on, kiddo," she said. "Me, I just like having a lot of laps to choose from. These demos are great – nobody minds when you sit on them, they give you lots of pats and soak up Carl's wisdom like sponges. It's win-win!"

And Lulu trotted off to find out just what was on the menu for lunch at Carl's.

Chapter Six

Winter followed autumn and the temperature dropped. Everyone made sure they wasted no time mounting their horses and getting them moving when the wind whipped around the outdoor school and the frost twinkled in the sunlight. The cold air caused the horses to shiver, and they looked for any excuse to spook and dive across the arena in mock horror, keeping their riders on their toes until their muscles were working and warm. Carl was sympathetic to the horses' behaviour in the cold and he stamped his own chilled feet as he taught his pupils, sipping hot water infused with lemon to keep warm. Had Brook Mill been situated in a warmer climate, a lemon grove may well have sprung from all the discarded lemon slices which littered the ground at the upper end of the outdoor school where Carl stood.

Blueberry asked Lulu whether Carl was putting on weight, he looked so much bigger during the winter months as he stood in the cold, giving advice to his riders and observing the progress of his pupils, human and equine. He hadn't seemed any heavier when he had ridden him, so Blueberry was puzzled.

"It's just layers!" grunted Lulu, who often appeared on the yard in a natty dog coat to keep chills at bay. Even in the coldest weather she still curled up on one of the seats next to Carl, making sure she snuggled into the thickest blankets to stay warm so she could keep abreast of each horse's progress and Carl's thoughts.

"Layers of what?" asked Blueberry, a disturbing image of a tower of fat popping into his mind.

"Carl's wearing more clothes," snorted Lulu. "Haven't you noticed that although his top half has expanded, his legs don't look any different? He's just wearing plenty of thick, padded clothes to keep warm."

Blueberry felt silly. He should have known that – hadn't Lydia changed his night rug to a thicker one now the weather was particularly cold? She even bandaged his legs at night when the frost crept along the top of his half-door and dusted the branches of the trees. When the temperature plummeted, the horses' water buckets and drinkers were checked regularly throughout the day, and the yard was inspected for patches of ice which could cause the horses to slip. Blueberry's breath came out in greater clouds during these cold days, and when he went out in the field with Orange, a low-lying mist sometimes hid their legs from view, which meant they took on the appearance of fairy horses, floating on clouds.

The guinea fowl were too small to be seen above the mist when it was there, but Blueberry could hear them as they bobbed along, more nervous than ever as they were shrouded in fog.

"Where are you?"

"I'm over here."

"Oh, there you are… on no, that's a stone."

"Ouch, what are you doing?"

"Sorry, didn't see you."

"What on earth is that!!!"

"It's just me. I think."

"I can't see my legs! Oh my goodness, someone's stolen my legs!"

"And mine!"

"Ahhhh, none of us has legs!"

"What are we going to do without legs?"

"I need my legs!"

And then the mist would clear momentarily, enabling all the guinea fowl to see that their legs were still there which, if they'd thought about it, was obvious as they were all still using them as they walked along. Not for the first time, Blueberry was glad he hadn't been born a guinea fowl.

It was on one such day, after Blueberry had been brought back in from the field and was tucking into his haynet, when he heard Orange neighing. Never wanting to miss anything, he quickly turned to look out over his door to see what was causing him to call. The yard was quiet, the grooms were all busy either riding, washing off horses or tidying the muck heap. Orange was looking down the driveway and Blueberry followed his gaze. There, sauntering lazily along the drive inside the main gates was a small, ginger cat. Its stride suggested it owned the place and its tail was held straight up, waving softly like a flag in a breeze.

"Clyde!" gasped Blueberry.

"He's back," said Orange – who had been quite anxious about Clyde's disappearance as he hated anything out of place or things left unexplained.

The ginger cat strolled into the yard where he was pounced on by his sister, Bonnie, who gave him a sound scolding. Where had he been? Why hadn't he told her where he was going? Had he been locked in someone's shed or outhouse? Was he all right?

"He looks fine," said Orange, and Blueberry noted that the ginger cat's tummy was just as round and his coat was just as shiny as they had been the day he disappeared.

"Stop making such a fuss," said Clyde, hopping up onto the concrete around one of the ornamental trees and sitting down gently, winding his tail neatly around him as though he had never been anywhere.

"Lydia has been so worried about you," Blueberry told him.

"No need," replied Clyde, blinking slowly. "I was fine."

"She's going to be pleased to see you," said Orange.

Pleased didn't adequately describe Lydia's

54

reaction when she walked onto the yard and caught sight of the cat she had thought lost. She dropped the grooming kit she'd been carrying and scooped Clyde up in her arms – much to Clyde's disgust.

"Where have you been?" she cried, hugging the cat to her and bursting into tears. Horrified at such a display of affection Clyde wriggled free, leaping from her arms and back up the tree, from where he looked down at her with his tail twitching. He was not impressed by his home-coming celebration.

Later that evening, when everyone had gone to bed, Blueberry spotted Clyde in the yard searching for any nocturnal creatures which might provide sport.

"Why did you go away?" Blueberry asked, wondering why anyone would want to leave Brook Mill when it was such a wonderful place to live.

"Why?" asked Clyde, staring at Blueberry with his large, amber eyes. "Why? Why not?"

"But everything you could want is here," replied Blueberry, not understanding Clyde at all. When he had been sent away, Blueberry found he couldn't wait to get back. Then something occurred to him. "Did someone *take* you away?" he asked.

"Of course not," said Clyde, lifting a front

paw and giving it a lick before shaking it and replacing it on the ground. "I just needed some space, that's all."

Blueberry's mind whirled. He still didn't understand. There was plenty of space at Brook Mill – especially for the cats who could go anywhere they pleased, even up in the high places like the top of the hay barn and the roof of the stable yard. Blueberry could feel his chin start to tremble.

"Cats are natural explorers," explained Clyde. "We need our freedom. We're not like the dogs (he spat out the word dogs, as though he couldn't get it out of his mouth quickly enough), who follow the humans around as though they're attached to them. And we're not like you horses – no offence – who are content to live in a stable or a field and let the humans ride you. Cats belong to no-one. Cats are their own bosses. Cats are free spirits."

With that explanation, which didn't help Blueberry at all, Clyde sashayed out of the yard and disappeared into the gloom of the trees, exercising his right to be a free spirit.

The following day, when Blueberry happened to mention to Lulu his conversation with Clyde, the little dog was dismissive.

"Free spirit indeed!" she snorted. "Cats are just ungrateful, they never show any appreciation of the hospitality Carl and the others have given them. Both Bonnie and Clyde were feral kittens without a home when Carl took them in. Feral cats and kittens," Lulu explained, seeing Blueberry's puzzled look (which wasn't just about his confusion about feral cats, but partly because he was kicking himself for mentioning Clyde at all, knowing Lulu's open and undisguised low opinion of cats in general), "have been born in the wild so have none of the social graces with which some – and only some, mind – domestic cats are blessed. They're not wild cats – oh no, they have domestic moggy parentage, usually escaped domestic cats, whose action further demonstrate a cat's lack of gratitude. Feral means they act wild, they think they're wild, but they're not really. They're nothing so exotic. No wonder Clyde's warbling on about being a free spirit. Totally up himself! I bet you," Lulu continued, narrowing her one eye, "that the reason he won't tell you where he's been is because it's boring and run-of-the-mill. It's so much more interesting to keep it a secret so we'll imagine all sorts of fantastic adventures – as if we had the time or the inclination!"

"Are any horses feral?" asked Blueberry, desperate to move Lulu away from the subject of the cats which he had initiated and now bitterly regretted.

"Yup, lots," said Lulu.

Blueberry was surprised. "Tell me more about them," he said.

So Lulu explained about the mustangs in the USA, descended from escaped domestic horses taken to the country by the Spanish conquistadors, and the Australian brumbies, who also ran wild but were descended from settlers' horses, no horses being native down under. The only true wild horse, Lulu told him, was the ancient Asiatic Wild Horse, which was now back in its native homeland after being reintroduced from horses bred in zoos after becoming extinct in the wild.

"Feral horses aren't like our Exmoor or New Forest ponies," Lulu explained. "They live out on the moors and in the forest, but they have owners. They're not wild and they're not feral, either. They just have a huge area to roam around and do what they like in, instead of living in a small field or a stable, and being ridden."

Blueberry took it all in. He had no idea about Exmoor or New Forest ponies. He realised, with a deep sigh, that there were always going to be things he didn't know, or understand. He decided that although he would continue to learn from Lulu it would be better if he concentrated on being a dressage horse. That, he thought, was difficult enough and quite enough to be getting on with. He wondered whether he would like to be a feral horse, or one living on Exmoor or the New Forest, wherever they were, but he decided that although it would be great to be able to graze all the time, he doubted feral horses were trained to perform dressage and that, as far as Blueberry was concerned, was the deal-breaker.

"I don't know how you know so much, Lulu," said Blueberry, gravely.

Lulu managed to look modest and superior at the same time. "Well," she said, her nose in the air, "I pay attention and pick things up. I find television is particularly useful."

Blueberry wanted to ask her to elaborate further on what television was and whether he might be able to get one, but he remembered his decision to concentrate on dressage and thought better of it.

So nobody ever found out where Clyde went. And Blueberry thought that Lulu was right, the cat's silence did seem to make the mystery more interesting and enigmatic – not to mention how much it annoyed Lulu. Thinking about it as he ate his hay in his stable that night, when all the yard was quiet and it was a good time for a little brown horse to go over the day's events and ponder on them, Blueberry reached the conclusion that cats and dogs seemed very intolerant of the way each saw the world and lived in it. Each had little time for the other and it didn't seem to occur to either of them that although they lived their lives differently, they could still accept those differences and be friends – or at the very least, be polite to each other. Blueberry didn't understand it; he and Lulu got on, he and Clyde got on. Why couldn't Lulu and Clyde get on? Wouldn't that just be much nicer for everybody?

All the wondering about the two species made Blueberry's head ache. He decided he'd leave the dog and cat to get on with it and just continue to be friends with both. He had enough to think about, after all.

Chapter Seven

Winter followed autumn, spring followed winter and it wasn't long before the horses welcomed the long, warm days of summer. Blueberry hadn't been idle during those months. He had been to several competitions with Carl and was looking forward to more. He was so happy to be ridden by Carl, he knew he could achieve anything he put his mind to with him in the saddle.

The dressage calendar is crowded with competitions and Blueberry found himself once more at the Badminton Young Dressage Horse of the Future, where he had triumphed the previous year when he had been only four years old, beating all the other four- and five-year-old horses earmarked for future champions. The sights, the smells, the sounds of the place were unmistakable, and Blueberry recognised where he was and he knew what he had to do. Something which was very different this year, however, was the weather. It had rained solidly for days beforehand and everywhere was soaking wet. The ground was muddy, the horses glistened in the downpours and everyone skidded and slipped on the wet grass. There seemed to be mud everywhere.

This year, Blueberry was in the five-year-old group, and the pressure was on; could he achieve the double and take the title for a second year or would another up-and-coming four-year-old steal the crown?

As Lucy, who was once again the groom on this outing, legged Carl up into the saddle, Blueberry remembered last year's comments from the other horses who had mistaken him for a Pony Club entry. He had shown them, he thought. Even so, he couldn't stop a pang of uncertainty creeping into his mind. He could see the other horses trotting around as they warmed up, and the little brown horse was once again aware that they all towered over him. Throughout the winter, Blueberry had hoped he would grow. He had heard Carl say that some horses were late developers, that all horses grew in fits and starts, rather than a steady increase but here, amongst the other horses, Blueberry could tell he was still small by comparison.

Blueberry dreaded warming up with the other equine competitors but, because of the weather and being keen to avoid the slippery grass, Carl headed him out to the quiet road by the side of the showground and it was there that he put his mount through his paces. It was weird warming up on the road, but Blueberry tried hard to concentrate, trying not to take too much notice of the sound of his hooves singing out on the tarmac as Carl tuned up the little brown horse, ready for his test.

Squelching their way back to the showground, Lucy gave Blueberry a wipe over with a stable rubber, and polished the mud from Carl's boots as they waited to be called. Blueberry watched as a dark bay horse walked out after his test, his head low, his rider looking pleased. Feeling a nudge from his own rider, Blueberry carried Carl into the arena and the pair performed in front of the judges. It was a good test; Blueberry was sure of it. He had felt Carl's confidence, felt the sureness of his aids and positive nature of his attitude, felt his own body moving as he'd been trained and performing the movements asked with a lightness he knew was required. It all seemed to flow so easily with Carl in his saddle and Blueberry felt sure he had done well. Carl and Lucy seemed delighted with his performance and he tucked into the sugar lumps offered and listened to them discussing the test. Good here, a breath-taking moment recovered there, a brilliant part somewhere else.

Later, he found out he had done better than all the other horses and was the winner of the five-year-old class! Blueberry remembered from the competition last year that they would need to go into the arena again, to see which horse from the four- and five-year-old winners the judge thought had star quality, and who would win the overall prize. Everyone in the Carl camp was thrilled when Blueberry was declared the overall winner for the second year running, and the little brown horse seemed to grow a hand taller in his final lap of honour with Carl. He was so happy! His success was continuing but, best of all, he was being ridden by Carl in his competitions. He and Carl were a team! He couldn't wait to share his thoughts with Lulu that evening, but because the weather got even worse and flooded the roads around the showground where Blueberry had warmed up earlier, getting home seemed impossible. Luckily, Lucy's family lived close by, so Carl took his horses there and they all stayed for a few days.

"It was great fun," Blueberry told Lulu when he eventually got home. "It was interesting to make some new friends and Lucy's family made a real fuss of me. It's good to be home, though, and I couldn't wait to tell you all about it."

"It sounds like you had a big adventure," Lulu said. She was happy to see her friend again and hear all about his success.

"It's all coming true, Lulu," sighed Blueberry, "my dream of becoming a top dressage horse, of being ridden in my tests by Carl. It's so wonderful when he rides me, it's as though we're that centaur thing you spoke about. I feel there is nothing I can't do, no movement I can't tackle and no test I can't perform well."

Lulu was strangely quiet. Usually she was full of support for her friend and encouraged his aspirations. This time, however, she just said how glad she was for him and no more.

Lulu knew that Carl was still searching for that special rider to take Blueberry further in his career and realised Carl's plans didn't include competing on the little brown horse for much longer. What could she say? There was no need to dash his hopes so cruelly, Lulu decided. Better to wait and see who would be riding him – and who knew, they might just be brilliant, and Blueberry might just love them as much as he loved Carl. It was possible, Lulu told herself, firmly. So firmly, she almost believed it. She just hoped Blueberry wouldn't lose heart when the new rider was found, and the little brown horse realised that his dream was to take a different road. She hoped it with all her heart.

Chapter Eight

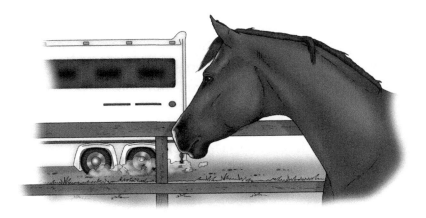

During the next few weeks Blueberry eagerly awaited his chance to compete more with Carl. Only now it was always Uti who was led out to the horsebox whenever Carl went to a competition. Once, twice, three times Blueberry counted. The horsebox returned with rosettes, Uti had been successful. When the horsebox trundled out of the yard for the fourth time with Uti on board and Carl in the cab, Blueberry felt his heart contract and his breathing shorten.

"Are you all right?" asked Orange, concerned

for his friend. He was the one who usually suffered from anxiety, not his confident and ambitious friend.

"Er, yes, of course," said Blueberry. But he wasn't. He was feeling something unfamiliar in his heart, something that he couldn't shake off, something that stayed with him day and night – especially at night. When the yard was quiet and darkness fell, Blueberry couldn't stop the feeling growing like the grass in the field. It was making him crazy.

"Okay kiddo," Lulu said one day, sitting down inside Blueberry's stable and giving him a knowing look with her one eye, "something is up and I need you to tell me what it is."

"It's nothing," Blueberry replied. Lulu took a look at his half-full haynet hanging in the corner. Usually Blueberry gobbled up every scrap then asked for more. Lydia had noticed, too. She had taken Blueberry's temperature, felt his heart rate and was keeping an eye on his whole demeanour, but she couldn't find anything physically wrong with her charge. Lulu knew the problem was in the little horse's head and heart. In her own heart, Lulu was sure she knew what Blueberry's problem was – but it went deeper than she thought.

"I think I know what it is," sighed Blueberry, knowing that if he had to tell someone, it would

68

be Lulu. If anyone could help him, his friend could. "Carl hasn't ridden me in a competition since the Badminton Young Horse of the Future. I did well, I won the whole class, but he hasn't competed with me since."

"He will do, I'm sure," said Lulu, not sure what else to say and almost certain she was wrong.

"He won't," wailed Blueberry. "He's too busy competing with Uti. I had so hoped to be Carl's horse, to be ridden in competitions by him, but it's Uti he's chosen. I can't bear it. I must have done something wrong. Carl must be disappointed with me but I can't think why, or what I've done. Do you know what it is, Lulu?"

"You haven't done anything wrong, I know it!" said Lulu, firmly. "Carl is very pleased with you, and thinks a great deal of you and what you've achieved so far. You mustn't blame yourself."

"Then he must think more of Uthopia than me. Uti must be much better than I am."

"Do you think it's Uti's fault?" asked Lulu.

Blueberry looked crestfallen. "No, not really," he sighed, knowing his friend had no say in where he went for competitions, or who rode him. "I'm not blaming Uti, although I'm finding it difficult to like him any more. I feel he's not my friend if he's the one Carl wants to ride, even though I know Uti hasn't changed. It's me who has changed, me who has the problem. I don't want to feel this way about him."

"Hmmm," said Lulu, seeing the extent of Blueberry's woes. He had been friends with Uti, he had looked up to him, but this situation was driving a wedge between the two horses. She realised this feeling Blueberry had was one he hadn't experienced before.

"Listen kiddo," began Lulu, kindly, "what you're feeling is called jealousy – the green-eyed monster. You badly want what you see Uti has, Carl as his rider. It seems to you that Uti has taken Carl from you. It's understandable that you feel like this, but you know Uti hasn't had anything to do with the decision making. All the horses want to be ridden by Carl and you know that Carl has always been worried that you're just not quite big enough for him to compete."

"I can't grow any more!" cried Blueberry. "It isn't fair!" The green-eyed monster that Lulu said he had inside him seemed to be taking over even as he spoke about his jealousy of Uti. He imagined it writhing around like a dragon, its wings fanning the fire it breathed into his heart. How did it get there? How could he get rid of it?

"No," agreed Lulu, "it isn't fair, but that's the

way it is. Jealousy is a horrible emotion and it eats away at you. You need to get a handle on it and stamp it out of your heart, however difficult that might be, because if you don't it will poison you. You'll never be free to perform brilliant dressage if you have jealousy in your heart because it will seep into your bones, tighten your muscles and cripple your performance. A dressage horse needs to have freedom of spirit and wings in his soul if he's to rise above the competition and be the best. You have to control this emotion – or it will control you. It's jealousy that's your enemy, kiddo, not Uti."

Lulu thought of the times when she had felt the raw emotion of jealousy. She had felt it when Willow had arrived, when any of the other dogs came to live at Brook Mill. She had seen it often, though, and had learned that just because there were other dogs in Carl's life, it didn't mean they replaced her. There was room in Carl's heart for all the dogs. He still loved her, she knew, and she had grown secure knowing that to be true. Lulu realised that the jealousy Blueberry felt was new to him, and therefore very intense. She hoped he would be able to get past it and not let it destroy his talent and demolish all he had built in his dressage career so far.

Blueberry thought hard, knowing what Lulu said made sense. He thought about the jealousy dragon inside and how this new, raw emotion made him feel. It made him feel ill, he thought. He knew, deep down, that Uti wasn't against him, he knew Carl wanted the best for him. But still it was hard not to be eaten up by the whole misery of how he was feeling, and how envious he was that Uti was competing with Carl when he wanted it to be him.

"I know you're right, Lulu," said Blueberry, "and I don't want this monster to stay inside me. It's horrible. I'll do my best to do as you say. I'll try my hardest to keep my friendship with Uti. I just wanted this so badly, you know, competing with Carl. When he's riding me I feel I dance almost like The Silver Dancer. None of the other riders make me feel that way."

"Of course they don't," agreed Lulu. "None of the other people who ride you are Olympic riders."

Blueberry forgot his jealousy for a second as his curiosity took over. "What do you mean? What's an Olympic rider?"

"Of course," said Lulu, "you don't know, do you, so where shall I start? You've only been to a few home competitions so far…"

"Home competitions?" interrupted Blueberry, confused. "But none of the competitions have been here, at Brook Mill."

"No, I don't mean that. When I say home

72

competitions, I mean competitions held in this country. But there are other, bigger, *international* competitions, sometimes held here, sometimes held in other countries. These competitions are big affairs, much more important than you've been to so far. They are called international competitions because competitors and their horses travel from other countries, all over the world, to compete against each other."

"When can I go to these?" asked Blueberry, thinking it sounded very grand and just the sort of thing he would love to do. He had travelled back and forth from his first home in Holland to Brook Mill in England, and some of the horses at Carl's had come from other countries so he knew there were more lands over the sea.

"You can't just go," explained Lulu. "Each country enters a team – three or four horses at most – selected by the equestrian governing body of each country. To be selected, each horse and rider has to prove they have a chance of winning against the other countries, so they need to be the best of the best, with a proven record of wins under pressure."

"So it's hard to get selected?" asked Blueberry.

"Very, very hard," agreed Lulu, glad that Blueberry's interest seemed to be diverting his jealous thoughts to something more positive. "And one of the most important of these international competitions, one of the hardest to be selected for, is the Olympic Games. They are held every four years and all the countries in the world enter and want to win. The winning horses and riders are the best in the whole world."

"Do you think I'll ever be good enough to be selected?" asked Blueberry, deciding that to go to an Olympic Games was now on his list of ambitions. In fact, it was at the very top of the list.

"Maybe, if you work hard. But no matter how hard you work you still have to be lucky because as well as getting top marks at the most important competitions and impressing the selectors you need to stay fit, travel well and prove to be a good team player who can really perform when the pressure is on. It's true of riders, too, and Carl has already competed at several Olympic Games with different horses. That's what I meant when I said he's an Olympic rider," Lulu continued. "He's one of the top dressage riders in the world, so it's not surprising you feel very different when he rides you."

Blueberry thought for a moment. "When are the next Olympic Games?" he asked.

"Next year in Beijing, that's on the other side of the world – but don't hold your breath, kiddo," Lulu warned him, "you're nowhere near ready to be thinking about being selected. You've never even been to any other international competitions or even competed in a Grand Prix. The Grand Prix tests are vital; the marks you get for your Grands Prix will determine whether you've reached the required standard. So you see, it's far too soon to imagine you might go to the next Games. I doubt you'll even be ready for selection for the following games, four years after Beijing, that's how tough it is.

"What other international competitions are there?" asked Blueberry, his heart sinking. It seemed that the road to the top in dressage got longer and longer the more he learned.

"There are the World Championships and the European Championships," said Lulu, her head on one side as she remembered them all. "And then there are other competitions held in other countries that give the horses and riders experience at competing at international level. But these big competitions are for experienced horses, and you'll need to be working at Prix St Georges and Grand Prix standard before you go to those. I wouldn't start worrying about them until you are performing canter pirouettes, passage and piaffe in your tests. You need to hone your craft in the smaller competitions, at the lower levels of dressage and work up to the big ones."

"So when I'm doing piaffe and passage, that's when I can go to the Olympic Games?" asked Blueberry.

"Only if you're good enough. Lots of horses can piaffe and passage, but they don't all get selected," said Lulu. "It's good to have the Games as your aim, but wanting to go doesn't mean you will. Anything might happen – there are no guarantees."

"Then I shall just have to work harder," Blueberry said, firmly.

"I believe you will," said Lulu. "And I believe you might just make it kiddo."

"Thanks Lulu," said Blueberry. Lulu's explanation of Carl's Olympic rider status and the international dressage competitions had shifted his focus away from his thoughts about Uti, if only for a few moments. Then the dragon inside him breathed more fire.

"Lulu, do you think Uti will go to the next Olympic Games?"

"No, he's nowhere near ready either," said Lulu, firmly.

Blueberry let out the breath he'd been holding and thought hard about what Lulu had told him. He realised he had to concentrate on his own career rather than waste his energy worrying about Carl's preference for Uti. But was that possible? But maybe, he thought, unable to quite believe that his dream of competing with Carl might be over, if he worked really hard then Carl would take *him* to the Olympic Games. If he was better than Uti, surely Carl would want to ride him after all. He had to try, it seemed like a plan which might just work. Blueberry decided he wouldn't mention it to Lulu. He couldn't bear it if she thought his plan wasn't worth trying. He had to cling to his belief.

"I'm here for you, kiddo, you know that," said Lulu. "Why don't you finish your hay – Lydia is worried about you, you know. And then you can tell me again how you won the Badminton Young Dressage Horse of the Future again, and don't you leave anything out, I want to hear every *single* detail."

Blueberry tugged at his haynet. The green-eyed jealousy dragon felt like it was waiting there inside him, waiting to be fired up again whenever he saw Uti leave for a competition with Carl. Lulu was right, he had to conquer this monster, he couldn't face the thought of carrying it around for ever. Besides, there was still the hope that Carl would compete with him if he worked hard enough, if he were chosen for the Olympic Games. As the last wisps of hay disappeared between his lips, the little brown horse cast his mind back to his last big competition success and he began to tell Lulu all about it, right from the moment he left the yard.

Lulu settled down with her nose on her paws and prepared to ask questions in all the right places. Her friend needed her more than ever and she wouldn't let him down.

Chapter Nine

Blueberry had learned that equine and human movements at Brook Mill ebbed and flowed like the oceans. People had days off – he always missed Lydia when she took hers – and for several weeks a year she disappeared on something called a *holiday*. Of course, all the horses went to shows, to demonstrations and, sometimes, they went to a new home. Pupils came for lessons, students arrived, stayed for a while and left, moving on to other jobs, other positions in the horse world. One day a new pupil arrived for a lesson with Carl. Carl remembered seeing her ride when he had been asked to help select talented riders for the World Class Performance Programme. This initiative had already helped several young riders along the pathway to international competition, and Britain's future dressage successes depended on spotting young riders who might posses the talent to represent their country in European, World and Olympic competitions in the future.

The girl had made an impression on him. She rode particularly well, her horse was schooled to a very high standard and her questions to Carl at the end of the day had come thick and fast, showing a keenness for her craft. The lesson he gave her now reminded Carl why he had been so impressed with her attitude, and with one of his grooms on holiday, he asked whether she would like to stay for a few days to help out, an offer the girl readily accepted. A few days' experience at Brook Mill was not something to be turned down!

Blueberry noticed the girl on the yard. Slender and fair-haired, she was keen to learn and worked hard so when Carl told her she was riding the little brown horse in a schooling session, Blueberry's ears twitched back and forth, eager to please this new rider. Carl watched the pair with interest. This girl was a strong rider and Blueberry, Carl knew, was inclined to be strong, too – especially in his mouth. He was so eager in his lessons, keen to get on and do everything his riders asked, he sometimes forgot himself and ignored his rider's rein aids. Good riders don't just use their reins to slow down, they use their seat, too, and this was particularly important for anyone riding Blueberry if they didn't want to be towed all around the arena, as many of the students had found to their cost! The little brown horse wasn't right for everyone, and some of the students found him difficult to sit to, especially in his rolling, ground-covering and bouncy canter which often caught them unawares – they were along the long side of the school in fewer strides than they had expected. Blueberry's canter was so big his riders often had problems controlling and collecting him.

This girl, however, was strong in her seat and wasn't fazed by Blueberry's canter. The pair seemed to like and understand each other from the get-go. Instead of fighting the little brown horse, the girl sat still and held him back with her seat, encouraging him not to rush but to control and contain his energy so that he bounced along like a rubber ball, ready to ping in any direction, at any pace, the moment she asked him.

Blueberry felt good under this girl and he could feel her confidence and excitement flowing through her hands, her seat and her legs. His own legs came up higher under his body, his neck arched more, his back was supple, his muscles felt like they were stretching and contracting with ease. This girl wasn't intimidated by his big paces and boundless enthusiasm and she seemed to enjoy the way he bounced around, eager to learn as much as anyone could teach him. There was solidness to her seat that Blueberry appreciated and it had a lot to do with the way she breathed.

Some of the students took short, hurried breaths, holding the air in their chests which caused tiny movements in the saddle. This girl breathed like Carl, deep in her diaphragm. This lowered her centre of gravity, making her seat more stable, her upper body still. Blueberry didn't understand why the breathing was so important but it made a huge difference to how he felt when he carried his rider. With this girl on his back Blueberry felt almost as he did when Carl rode him, and he could have performed dressage all day!

Watching the pair of them from the end of

82

the outdoor arena, Carl nodded his head in appreciation. Yes, Blueberry and this girl made a good pair. The girl grinned widely as she felt the amazing paces and power beneath her, and Carl could see how confident Blueberry felt with her. And then, suddenly, he saw something else in this young, enthusiastic young girl. The girl called Charlotte, who was getting such a positive tune out of Blueberry, reminded Carl of himself when he was her age. This girl, Carl instinctively felt, had the potential to ride at Grand Prix level, the highest in dressage, and for a second Carl imagined her riding Blueberry in an international arena, dancing for fun. Could he have found the right rider for Blueberry? Was he watching now the rider he had been searching for?

Chapter Ten

Brook Mill was always busy with people coming and going. Blueberry recognised a lot of them; the farrier was a regular visitor, checking all the horses' feet and replacing shoes, as was the woman who gave the horses a stimulating massage. There was the back person – who checked that the horses had no problems with their spines which could influence their paces or cause lameness – and there were regular visits from the feed merchant who delivered supplies of the horses' hard feed, as well as the hay lorries and the bedding deliveries. And, of course, there were pupils with their own horses, and a few respected ex-competition riders well-known to Carl, who came to hack out the horses for fun.

But there was one woman who, as far as Blueberry could tell, fell into none of the above categories. Tall and blonde, she sometimes visited with her son and young daughter, but more often alone. When she did visit, she always dropped by Blueberry's stable for a chat and spent more time with him than with any of the other horses. Being a friendly sort, Blueberry was happy to pass the time of day with this woman, who he heard Carl call Roly, and he was even happier when she offered him a tit-bit or two, stroking his forehead and talking gently to him. She and Carl often stood outside Blueberry's stable, talking about him. Curious about her, Blueberry knew who he could go to for answers to his questions.

"Roly?" asked Lulu. "Ahhh, yes, Roly is a very important person – to you," she said. She had been on her way to the outdoor school where she could hear Carl teaching, but Blueberry had stopped her as she'd trotted past his stable.

"Important to me?" asked Blueberry. "Why?"

"Hmmm, how can I put this…" Lulu mused,

her muzzle wrinkling up as she sought out the right words. "You know you're Carl's horse," she began, noticing Blueberry nodding, "well Carl has only half of you now. The other half of you is Roly's."

Blueberry stared down the drive and wondered how he felt about that. "Which half?" he asked.

"Say again?" said Lulu.

"Which half of me is Roly's?" asked Blueberry. "Everything in front of my middle? Everything behind my middle? My top half? My lower half? My inside? My outside?"

"No, of course not!" exclaimed Lulu. "When I say she owns half of you; you can't divide yourself up. She and Carl share you – that's what I should have said."

"She never rides me," said Blueberry. "Carl does. Why doesn't Roly?"

"I don't know," said Lulu. "She just doesn't."

"They why does she want to share me?" asked Blueberry. The whole thing made no sense to him.

"You're not the only one, you know," said Lulu. "Lots of the horses have more than one owner. Some of them never ride, some hardly ever come and see them. It seems that some people just like having an interest in a competition horse. They like following their

86

progress and going to the shows. It's a great interest for them. Plus, it helps pay the bills. There are a lot of bills to pay in this dressage game, you know."

"Do you think she'll want to take me away?" asked Blueberry, suddenly fearful.

"No," said Lulu, firmly. "Roly wants you to be here, she enjoys sharing you with Carl and she won't be taking you anywhere. She's a partner, if you like, one of the team – a very important member of the team. You like her, don't you, she's nice, isn't she? She always has time to scratch a small dog behind the ears so she's pretty swell in my book," Lulu told him.

"Oh yes," agreed Blueberry, hastily. Roly *was* nice. He did like her. If Lulu thought she was important, Blueberry decided he'd be extra nice to her in future. So when she turned up again a few days later, Blueberry made sure he spent some time with his head over his half door, accepting the carrots or apples offered on her palm and taking an interest in his half-sharer. He hadn't realised she was an important member of the team so he was glad he'd asked Lulu about her, and even more glad he could show his appreciation by spending some time with her.

Chapter Eleven

Charlotte, the girl who had come for a few days to cover for a member of staff on holiday, never left Brook Mill. She became a permanent fixture at the yard, riding the young horses and, in particular, the little brown horse known as Blueberry. Carl had put together a combination that seemed to click. Blueberry was strong – both in his body and his mouth

– his natural exuberance making it difficult for some riders to cope with. Charlotte was a strong rider and instead of fighting against Blueberry, she shared his enthusiasm and as they learned more and more under Carl's tutorage, the pair grew in confidence as well as ability. With the advanced horses of Carl's to ride, Charlotte was able to learn from them and, in turn, teach Blueberry to expand his knowledge. Blueberry became wrapped up in his training, and was excited as he learned ever more advanced movements. But even the fact that he was learning so much and achieving his dream of dancing like The Silver Dancer, didn't erase the searing pain he felt whenever he saw Carl leave for a competition with Uti instead of him, and the dragon inside him began breathing fire into his heart once more.

Lulu, noticing when this happened, tried to spend time with her friend to keep his mind off his worries.

"Tell me what you've been doing with Charlotte," Lulu said to him one day. She had spotted Blueberry staring wistfully after the horsebox which had whisked Uti and Carl away to another competition.

"What? Oh, yesterday I did flying changes in canter for the first time," Blueberry told her, remembering his excitement as he changed canter lead in the outdoor school. Changing legs was easy when he was by himself in the field, but he had worked out what the aids Charlotte had given him had meant and he had managed to hesitate in mid-stride and twist his body slightly so he landed in canter on the opposite lead.

"Both legs?" asked Lulu. "Fore and hind?" It was quite common for inexperienced horses to change lead with their front legs only, the hind legs continuing in the original canter lead – but a successful change required both fore and hind legs to change together. If not, the resulting canter is known as disunited, which is unbalanced and uncomfortable for both horse and rider.

"Yes, both legs," said Blueberry. "I hoped I had given Charlotte what she had asked for and when she gave me pats and a fuss I knew I had got it right. I'll recognise the aid next time."

"The top horses can change lead at every stride," Lulu told him. "It looks fabulous, but it's very difficult. Charlotte will ask for fewer strides gradually and…"

"Do you think Carl will ever take me to a competition again?" Blueberry interrupted, breathlessly.

Lulu thought hard. She wanted to say what her friend longed to hear, that yes, Carl would compete with Blueberry. The trouble was, she knew that wasn't true and she respected the little brown horse too much to lie to him just to make him feel better now. It would only make things worse in the future when that which he most wished for didn't happen.

"Listen kiddo," Lulu said gently, "you have to move on. You have what it takes to be a top dressage horse and you mustn't let anything destroy that dream. You like Charlotte, don't you?"

Blueberry nodded.

"You're enjoying your schooling together?"

Blueberry sighed, knowing his question wasn't going to get the answer he longed for.

"Carl's still competing Uti," Blueberry said, lowering his head. "He's never going to ride me in competition again, is he?"

"You know, I've a feeling you may be able to achieve your dream with Charlotte, if you really want to," Lulu told him. "Think about it, kiddo. The path to the top isn't always straightforward and you may be presented with several forks in the road before you get there. Don't let your disappointment about Carl ruin your chances. Work with Charlotte and you will be a top international dressage horse, I'm sure of it. Dreaming of what might have been, and concentrating on what you haven't got, instead of what you have, will only prevent you from progressing at all. Why not give it all you've got with Charlotte?"

Blueberry thought hard. His chin wobbled with effort. He knew what Lulu was saying was true and he respected her advice. The horrible dragon still rose in his heart whenever he saw Carl taking Uti to a show instead of him. Could he really achieve his dream with Charlotte? He knew he had to try.

"Okay Lulu," said Blueberry, hoping that by saying what he needed to say, he would believe it and be able to work towards it. "I'll try my hardest. Charlotte's nice, I like her, she's a brilliant rider and we work well together. We'll show them all!"

"Good plan!" said Lulu, and she snuggled up under Blueberry's manger while he chewed on his hay, in a demonstration of solidarity. There were always setbacks on the way to success, she thought. She had seen it happen with other horses at Brook Mill, and other people, too. It was a test of character. Some people thought successful horses and people were lucky, and that luck and wanting to achieve their dream was enough to take them to the top. But Lulu had seen how success was earned by hard work and the ability to pick oneself up after disappointments – physical and mental – and find a way through the maze of setbacks to achieve a dream. Lulu had a feeling this wasn't the only hurdle Blueberry would have to overcome if he were to become a top dressage horse. But how he tackled and overcame this problem, now, was crucial to how he might overcome future disappointments. So far, she thought, Blueberry was coping well; every setback was teaching him something, and hardening his resolve.

True to his word, Blueberry tried his hardest to concentrate on his work with Charlotte and it certainly paid off. The pair went to several outings during the summer where they did well in various dressage tests. On these outings, Blueberry was so interested in what was going on, and so wrapped up in performing as well as he could, he had little time to reflect that he wasn't being ridden by Carl and the jealousy dragon seemed to stay asleep inside him. Carl was always there, keeping a close eye on the progress of his two pupils and guiding them every step of the way. They were both young, and they needed all his experience behind them if they were to achieve their dreams. He and Charlotte discovered that the little brown horse became so excited at competitions, and so keen to show off his paces, that their warm-up routine needed to be thought out carefully if Blueberry was to arrive at his test poised to perform well, without blowing up and bouncing all over the place.

Carl decided that Charlotte needed to ride Blueberry twice in order to warm up well. It took a lot of work and effort – and it had to be timed right so that Blueberry wasn't fed up or tired (nor Charlotte, for that matter!) as they went into the arena. The right balance was achieved when the little brown horse was calm and listening to his rider, rather than pinging around like a pinball machine, or looking around and deciding to do his own thing in the test. A dressage test is supposed to demonstrate not only how well the horse is schooled, how supple and correct in his paces he is, but also how well he listens to his rider and does exactly as they ask, when they ask. Blueberry tended to think he knew best if he hadn't had sufficient warm-up time!

Each progressive test was chosen to build confidence and judge the progress of training, and Carl was careful in his preparation, not wishing to overface Blueberry and Charlotte. Dressage horses and riders work their way through tests designed for each stage of training; Preliminary, Novice, Elementary, Medium, Advanced Medium and Advanced, before going on to Prix St Georges, Intermediate I and Intermediate II, where the more advanced movements are asked for. The ultimate test was the Grand Prix – and these are further sub-divided into National and International Grand Prix, which qualify for the Grand Prix Special and the Grand Prix Freestyle, where the riders devise their own tests including the most difficult required movements, to music of their choice.

Blueberry and Charlotte were currently competing at Novice level, even though their training at Brook Mill was more advanced, so that when they competed they were confident performing the movements required. All the further competition levels were still in the future for the little brown horse – but only if he proved he was good enough. But the thought of failing to achieve his goals was too hard to contemplate, and Blueberry was so determined to progress through the ranks – ranks he had little idea about yet – that he pushed the thought of failing out of his head. He was a dressage horse (didn't his winning rugs say so?) and reaching the top in dressage was what he had to do.

Chapter Twelve

There was always a buzz about the yard at Brook Mill as September approached because that was when the National Dressage Championships were held. Carl had planned each horse's competition progression throughout the year, and all his working horses had qualified to go to the Nationals in various classes – including Blueberry with Charlotte, who had qualified for the Novice Championship! Blueberry had no idea the contest was going to be so important but it was a big test for the little brown horse, especially as there was also the Shearwater Five-Year-Old Championship to ride for. The Nationals were a big thing for everyone at Brook Mill – they were held over four days, meaning that horses were coming and going all that time. All the grooms were busy getting the horses ready, packing all the equipment and tack in the horsebox and making sure all the horses which were not going were still looked after and ridden. They also had to avoiding treading on the dogs, who got under everyone's feet as they felt the buzz around the yard and were determined to be included. The cats, Bonnie and Clyde, upset by all the activity, made themselves scarce, only appearing at meal times. It was all a bit too much for them. They preferred a quiet life.

Lydia had made list after list, all pinned up in the tack room. They included the names of the horses who were going on each day, who was going with them, the timetable for each departure and who was responsible for running the yard and the essential jobs at home. The logistics were complicated, but everyone was used to it and knew which part they had to play.

The horses just had to do as bid – but the atmosphere was electric and they all picked up on it.

"It looks like I'm going," wailed Orange, as one of the grooms plaited his mane. His competitive career was coming along, apart from a few blips when he faltered in his tests, the distractions and his dislike of being watched and judged getting the better of his nerves. He, like Blueberry, was working at Novice level, and had qualified for his class at the Nationals. Unlike Blueberry, he was not looking forward to the experience.

"It must be a big show," said Blueberry, before realising that was the last thing Orange wanted to hear. "I mean, it's probably not *that* big a deal," he said, noticing his friend's pained expression.

"Are you two ready for the big time?" asked Willow, as he sauntered past. He had already gulped down a sandwich he'd found on the wall where one of the grooms had abandoned it in a distracted moment, and he had high hopes of discovering more bounty as the day progressed. His question didn't help Orange's nerves, although it did increase Blueberry's excitement level a notch or two.

Blueberry bounded up the horsebox ramp, keen to be off, and Orange dawdled up behind him. The journey wasn't a long one and soon Blueberry was tacked up at the showground and being ridden around by Charlotte in an attempt to get him relaxed and listening.

Blueberry recognised the showground; it was where he had won the Shearwater Four-Year-Old Championship the year before, and it was buzzing! The atmosphere was how he remembered, everyone was excited to be at the Nationals – Blueberry hadn't realised the show's significance last year – and all the horses looked in tip-top condition. It was hard to concentrate there was so much to see. Music blared out from loudspeakers, grooms ran to and fro, spectators walked about greeting each other and waving their programmes, their dogs straining on leads and reacquainting themselves with old friends. Blueberry suddenly missed Lulu. She had stayed at home this time, banned from coming on this mega busy occasion. There was enough for Lydia to think about without looking out for one very independent, one-eyed dog!

As usual, Blueberry could hear the other horses' comments as he and Charlotte warmed up.

"Careful, don't come too close to me, please!"

"I'm trying to shorten my stride, but this is all so exciting I don't think I want to!"

"Hey, Sam, I see you've got a new rider. How's that working out for you? She doesn't look as good as the last one!"

Carl stood by the fence, giving Charlotte instruction as she rode her mount around in preparation for the Novice Championship. Gradually, Blueberry's trot became steadier, his head lower as he concentrated more and listened to his rider.

"Don't let him fool us," said Carl. "He's still on his toes and he'll need another ride around just before the test."

Blueberry knew that to be true. He felt as though his hooves were made of rubber and he knew he could do better. But it was so difficult trying to concentrate when there was so much going on, so much to see, to smell, to hear! He was glad Uti wasn't with them so he didn't have to see Carl riding him around. Perhaps he was coming on another day, he thought with an intake of breath. He was working at a higher level, after all. Blueberry was excited to be at the Nationals, but he still felt jealous of his friend. Could he do as well this year with Charlotte in his saddle?

After further preparation in the warm-up arena, Carl declared his pupils ready for their test. They had timed it well and had to wait only a short time before being called into the

100

arena. Blueberry felt Charlotte gather up his reins, felt her legs tremble slightly at his sides, her breath rhythmic as usual – and yet not quite the same. She was confident, she knew what they had to do, but the excitement of the occasion still transmitted from her body, her legs, her hands, to her mount. The little brown horse tucked in his chin. He would need to concentrate very hard for the next few minutes. He vowed he wouldn't let Charlotte – or Carl – down.

The test went well; Blueberry could feel it. His transitions were spot on, his paces fluent, energetic yet controlled by his rider. His circles were accurate, his walk on a long rein relaxed. Blueberry listened intently to what Charlotte asked him to do and did it as well as he could, aware of the judges looking at him, awarding him marks. He wanted good marks and he made sure he did his best, which was easy to do as Charlotte rode him well and confidently. All too soon the test was over, Charlotte was steering him out of the arena and Lydia was offering him a sugar lump.

"Good job, the pair of you!" Carl enthused, knowing they stood a good chance of winning the competition. He was delighted with his pupils. Sure enough, their marks saw Blueberry and Charlotte head the line-up and canter their victorious lap of honour, to the astonishment of some the other horses, who had disregarded Blueberry as a serious threat, unfamiliar with his rider and certain such a small horse could not be much competition. It was the last time the opposition at home underestimated the little brown horse introduced over the loudspeaker as Valegro.

Everyone was in high spirits – the pairing had done brilliantly in their first big competition which set them up for further success for in the Shearwater Five-Year-Old Championship, where Charlotte and Blueberry once more achieved the highest marks, gaining more respect from the other horses and riders, not to mention the spectators, who realised they had just seen something special.

"You've done well," a black mare in the presentation line-up said, but before Blueberry could thank her, the black mare's tone changed. "But I've seen this happen before, and the more difficult work is yet to come. I've seen horses win at this level but when the work gets harder, and their riders ask for more collection and greater effort, they don't always maintain their brilliance."

"Take no notice of her, Valegro," said a bay gelding further down the line. "Most of us think you'll go on to even greater success, especially with Carl Hester training you and your promising new rider. Good luck!"

Blueberry's emotions see-sawed; at first he felt elation at his double success, then insecurity as he heard the words of the black mare, followed by determination and pride as the bay's encouragement lifted him again. Little did the black mare realise that her negative comments only served to fire up the little brown horse to greater effort. She had no idea of the determination inside Blueberry to be the best dressage horse he could be, no clue that he watched The Silver Dancer at night, dancing in ever-changing colours as the lights shone and of how this inspired the young horse to follow in its hoof prints.

It seemed to Blueberry that although his training was fun and consistent, and his confidence grew with every session Carl instructed Charlotte in his saddle, his emotions were all at sea. He loved winning, loved how he felt when he performed in the dressage arena, showing the judges and the audience how well he understood Charlotte's instructions and carrying out the movements as well as he possibly could. But a spiteful comment by another horse could plunge him into despair, especially if it was directed at his height because that was something he could do nothing about.

It drove him to work harder, to show everyone that he, Blueberry, was just as capable as the bigger horses.

And then there was the awful, unwelcome emotion that gnawed at his heart at unexpected moments – when he saw Carl riding Uti in a competition, when he caught sight of him schooling the stallion when Blueberry longed for Carl to be his rider. It caught him unawares, just when he thought he was getting to grips with it. That was the worst of the jealousy dragon that lurked inside him. He could fight his size, he could work as hard as he could, but this creature crept up within him and seized control of his feelings without warning – just when he thought he had it licked. He knew he had to learn to shake it off and send it packing.

Could he do that, he wondered. He had to. If he didn't, Blueberry knew it could hold him back from his dream. And that made him more determined than ever to fight the monster and chase it away. For good.

Chapter Thirteen

Blueberry's success as a five-year-old gave him tremendous confidence as he continued his training throughout the next year. He and Orange often discussed their schooling sessions, and helped each other when each found something challenging. Orange had a wobble with his tempi-changes (changing legs at canter) and Blueberry's advice helped him greatly.

"Don't think just about your fore-legs," Blueberry advised him. "If I do that, I sometimes concentrate so much on them, I forget the hind legs. Think of your legs on one side as a pair and then, if you are collected enough, and the power is all behind you, you'll change legs without thinking about it."

Orange reported back the next day how successful Blueberry's advice had been. "I love doing my tempi-changes now," he said. "I can change every four strides. How are you getting on with your rein-back?"

"Better!" said Blueberry. "I was a bit keen, like you said, and kept taking a step or two too many. But now I take a breath and step back more slowly and Carl and Charlotte seem very pleased."

Things were changing gradually – both at Brook Mill and in Blueberry's head, and this was reflected in how he had begun to refer to Carl and Charlotte in the same breath. He still wished Carl was riding him, but not so often now, and without the same wistfulness. The little brown horse was coming to realise that he and Charlotte made a great team. They were both strong – the horse in his mouth and his paces, the rider not only in her riding, but in her competitive and determined attitude – and they were learning fast. Blueberry seemed able to offer every movement Charlotte asked from him, enabling them to concentrate on honing their skills and perfecting their craft.

That year saw the pair successful in many championships, the main ones being the Winter Elementary Championship in April, and both the Elementary and Medium Championships at the National Dressage Finals in September. Blueberry also triumphed in the Shearwater Six-Year-Old Championship.

At each competition, Blueberry began to look forward not only to the tests themselves, but the reaction of the crowds afterwards. They applauded, they shouted, they waved. Blueberry realised the applause was for him and he looked around with interest at the presentations where he received his rosettes, a sash and, more often than not, a new rug, interested in what was going on around him. If the spectators appreciated his efforts, thought Blueberry, the least he could do was show them he had noticed, and he hoped his crowd-gazing as he walked around was correctly interpreted as his acknowledgement to them. He wanted so much to thank them for their support. He didn't quite realise just how impressed the dressage crowds were by this new partnership, how they loved to see the little brown horse called Valegro perform dressage so well, and with such ease.

"Are all those new rosettes in the tack room yours?" Willow asked him one autumn day, just after Blueberry had been clipped again. "You've won loads, now, haven't you?" the big dog observed.

"It's been a great year," agreed Blueberry. His mind often drifted back to his successes, and he liked nothing more than to think about them as he lay in his stable on winter evenings, listening to Lulu's breathing (and sometimes snoring!) as she slept under his manger, and wondering what he would learn with Charlotte in his next schooling session. It was during one of these quiet times when Blueberry realised he was looking forward to his schooling session with Charlotte the next day, instead of wishing that Carl would be riding him.

Oh, he thought, his chin wobbling with concentration, I *am* looking forward to it. I'm looking forward to schooling *with Charlotte*. I don't mind so much if it isn't Carl, I'm no longer *so* disappointed Carl's not riding me. After all, Carl is training me – he's training us, *together*. We're a successful team, Carl, Charlotte and me. And, he added, with surprise, I don't even mind so much about Carl competing Uti.

Blueberry had turned a corner as far as his jealousy was concerned. He lay down on his bed and drifted off to sleep, content that the green-eyed monster which had troubled him so badly, if not quite gone for good, was certainly fading away. This feeling felt lighter, it seemed to set him free. Blueberry's dreams that night were good ones, and he awoke feeling refreshed and ready to face the future.

Blueberry always enjoyed the routine at Brook Mill and, in particular, when the farrier came in his van. He could tell that the two men who trimmed the horses' hooves and fitted them with shoes were not quite equal – one was definitely the boss, who seemed to know everything about hooves and spent time discussing with Carl each horses' individual needs, hoof-wise. The other seemed to be a trainee, learning from the first, and it was always the trainee who removed Blueberry's shoes and gave them a preliminary trim, ready to be fitted with new shoes by the 'boss'. This was only after Lydia had trotted Blueberry up and down the yard while both men assessed his action. Blueberry didn't know it, but his farrier was a bit of a celebrity in the horse-shoeing world.

"Only the best for Carl's horses," explained Lulu. Blueberry couldn't help noticing that whenever the farrier's van pulled into the yard, all the dogs stopped whatever they were doing and sat in the yard, watching proceedings with the concentration of an audience at one of Carl's

)s. Blueberry couldn't understand why
.er all, it wasn't as though they could be
ᴜᴠ.ᴧees and go on to be farriers themselves.

"Okay, kiddo, here's how it is," began Lulu, keeping her one eye firmly fixed on the boss farrier as he set up his anvil on the yard, fetched his tray of tools and fastened his leather apron around himself to protect his clothes while the trainee began trimming Orange's hooves. "Firstly, the trainee is called an apprentice – he's learning how to be a farrier. It takes a long time to learn, and every trainee is apprenticed to a fully-trained farrier for that time."

"How long does it take?" asked Blueberry.

"Years and years," Lulu replied, not quite sure how many years, and hoping Blueberry wouldn't press her for an exact number. "It takes a farrier almost as long to learn his craft as it does a dressage horse to learn his," Lulu added.

Blueberry was astonished. There had to be an awful lot to learn about hooves.

Lulu could see he was impressed. "Yes, there's a lot they need to learn," she said, "and a lot going on in those hooves. If your hooves don't work, *you* don't work. It's vital your hooves are healthy, trimmed correctly, properly fitted with shoes which are tailored specifically to you, and that you stay sound. One slip with a hammer or a clench – that's a horseshoe nail – and you're out of action. Remember that old saying, *no foot, no horse*," she added.

Blueberry could see the importance of correct training for farriers, just as it was for dressage horses. Except that farrier training included the added responsibility for every horse's ultimate hoof health.

"But like most professionals," Lulu continued, "farriers don't just stop learning once they're qualified. There's always more to learn and the boss, well he's pretty hot stuff, farrier-wise. He specialises in shoeing performance horses – that's horses like you – and he's the official farrier for Team GB's dressage and show jumping teams…"

"What's Team GB?" asked Blueberry, feeling a bit stupid. No matter what Lulu told him, it seemed there were always more questions to ask.

"You don't really need to know that right now," said Lulu, who had been interrupted in mid-flow and was now trying to remember where she had got to. "Oh yes," she said, picking up her thread again, "your farrier is always in demand to give lectures on shoeing, and he carries out a lot of research. Caring for equine feet is one of those science-y things that you never know everything about, apparently."

"Is that why you and the other dogs watch so intently?" asked Blueberry, very impressed by his farrier's credentials. "You can appreciate fine workmanship?"

"Er, no," said Lulu, looking slightly embarrassed.

"Why do you do it, then?" asked Blueberry.

"Well, let's just say we like to tidy up after him," said Lulu, hoping that explanation would be enough for the curious brown horse. Of course, it wasn't – she knew, deep down, that it wouldn't be.

"Tidy up?" said Blueberry, his chin on the wobble.

"Oh, well, if you must know, we like to chew on the bits they trim off your hooves. They're not only deliciously smelly but rather tasty and chewy and, well, just nice to chomp on."

Blueberry looked down at his hooves. Then he looked across at the trainee – no, he remembered, the *apprentice* – trimming Orange's near fore. The dogs were all watching closely and when the apprentice threw the hoof-shaped piece onto the yard Willow pounced, grabbed it in his mouth, and sat down in the corner gnawing at it like a bone.

Blueberry thought uncomfortable thoughts. "Do you ever get the urge to nibble at my hooves *before* they're trimmed?" he asked.

112

"Of course not!" exclaimed Lulu, horrified. "As if! That would not only be rude it would be, well it would be... well anyway, we don't. Besides," she added, a twinkle appearing in her eye which went unnoticed by Blueberry, "we can't get to them when you're wearing shoes."

Blueberry's own eyes widened.

"I'm only joking!" said Lulu, realising she may have gone too far. Blueberry didn't get the joke at all. "And it's not as though you want those bits any more, do you? I mean, they're surplus to requirements so we are, if you think about it, *recycling*."

Blueberry decided he wouldn't think about it any more. Dogs, he thought, were very unlike horses. If the dogs had their claws trimmed he knew, without a doubt, that the last thing he would ever want to do is chew on them. He decided to concentrate on how important his farrier was, instead of what happened to the bits of his hooves he no longer needed. It was amazing that he had such a famous and highly qualified person in charge of his hooves, and he looked at the two men in a different light.

Chapter Fourteen

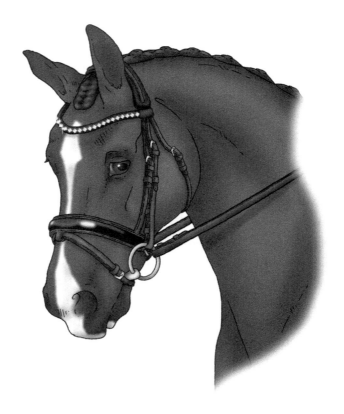

Blueberry's next big outing was at the Winter Championships in spring the following year where he emerged Medium Champion. At seven years old, he had finished growing and was a mature, well muscled horse performing all the dressage movements he would need in his Prix St Georges tests he would enter next year. But first, there were the National Championships, and Blueberry was the favourite to win the Advanced Medium Championship this year. With the Winter Medium Championship under their belts, it was as though the duo of Blueberry and Charlotte was unstoppable and could do no wrong.

Blueberry recognised the set-up as soon as the horsebox rolled onto the showground early in the morning. He remembered his successes the previous year and couldn't wait to show everyone how improved he was.

"Blueberry's test is one of the earliest," Carl reminded Lydia, who had got up almost in the middle of the night to get the horses ready. Now she had saddled Blueberry and was waiting for Charlotte to mount up and warm up.

"You haven't got much time," Carl warned her, as she steered an excited Blueberry to the practice arena to warm up. Blueberry recognised some horses from previous competitions. He could see riders who were confident, and others who were less confident looking pale and nervous. It was a chilly morning and the slight breeze felt like ice. Charlotte felt the power of the little brown horse beneath her as Blueberry pinged around the arena, full of himself.

"Five minutes!" shouted Carl, keeping an eye on the time. Why couldn't Blueberry's test have been in the afternoon? He was so fresh this morning and could have done with a lot more work before his test.

Charlotte steered Blueberry over to the arena where the horse and rider before them were finishing their test. Blueberry still felt lively under her, and she regretted the traffic which had held them up on the way. They always warmed up twice! But there was no more time, they were being called in to the arena.

Blueberry didn't feel fully relaxed. Usually, after being ridden around he felt ready for his test, alert but calm. Today he felt slightly on edge. What was that noise over there? Who was waving a flag about behind him? He tried to concentrate, knowing how important it was to settle down and do his best.

They began their test. Blueberry knew his trot was good, it felt excellent. How about his walk – no longer ONLY a seven or eight walk, he thought to himself, thinking back to the demonstration day at Brook Mill where he had vowed to improve the quality of his walk. And he had! Cantering now... he had to listen to Charlotte, she might ask for a transition to walk,

116

or ask for an extended pace or request that he went sideways for several strides…

Suddenly, there was a loud noise alongside the arena – someone had dropped something and the sound caught Blueberry's attention. What was that? For a second his attention shifted from being totally focused on Charlotte, to the noise. And then he realised Charlotte had asked him to change pace and he hadn't heard her. He was still cantering when she had asked him to trot, and now they were way past the marker. Was it too late to recover the situation?

It was. The moment had passed and the mark was lost. Blueberry did his best to concentrate for the rest of the test – but it was too late. Any mistake at this level was going to cost the pair the championship, and that was exactly what happened. It was the only championship they didn't win that year.

Blueberry wondered whether he would ever get over his disappointment. How could he have been so easily distracted? Lulu did her best to console him, telling him not to take it so hard, that Carl didn't blame the little brown horse but himself, knowing that if Blueberry had been warmed up more before the competition, things would have been different.

"One thing's for sure," Lulu told him, grimly, "it's a mistake which won't happen again!"

117

Chapter Fifteen

As Blueberry stood outside the arena at the National Dressage Championships the following year he couldn't help but be proud. Here he was, the little brown horse who everyone had thought was too small to go to the top in dressage, waiting to be called into the arena to begin his Prix St Georges test with Charlotte. This was a big test; to continue his career, to go on to greater things he had to demonstrate that he could carry out all the difficult movements included in the test. He had learned them thoroughly at home. He had done his best not just to learn them, but to carry them out correctly with grace, rhythm and that little extra which he recognised as being essential for a top dressage horse. He had to show the judges that he had flair, that he had style, that he had what it took to keep them looking at him, not wanting to draw their eyes away but enjoy every second of his performance. Could he do it? Was he ready?

The pressure Blueberry felt was not just about this one test. He was performing at Prix St Georges level – and Blueberry remembered that the movements in these tests were the basics of those required at international level. It would be his performance in these tests on which his dream of competing internationally depended.

Charlotte scratched his neck and whispered that he could do it, that she had every faith in him but also that they were to go in to that arena and have fun. She knew that enjoying what they did always lifted their performance. It was obvious to everyone watching which horses and riders carried out the movements mechanically, trying their hardest but feeling under pressure, and which horses and riders loved their work and put joy into every step, a true partnership. It was the joyful combinations which stayed in the mind and inspired others, turning the moves into a balletic, equine dance.

As Charlotte steered Blueberry into the arena the little horse felt excitement in his heart and he couldn't wait to show off. But he had to listen to his rider, to wait for her signals, feel her aids and the tiniest of body movements to tell him what he should be doing, and when. That was the most difficult thing of all.

As soon as they began the test Blueberry knew he and Charlotte were on fire! His extended trot covered the ground with power, but came back to a collected trot at the merest whisper of his rider's request. They flew across the arena sideways in half-pass before the extravagant tempi-changes, light and full of energy. The half canter pirouette was tricky – such a difficult movement where Blueberry had to pivot and step on one hind hoof, rhythmically turning in canter to describe a semi-circle in three to five steps, never losing the tempo – and then on again around the arena, demonstrating his training, showing everyone how he and Charlotte worked in harmony together, totally as one.

The test over, he felt Charlotte loosen the reins to allow him to stretch his neck. Had he done enough? Blueberry sensed his rider wasn't as happy as she could be. Had he been over zealous? Had the judges noticed he had got so carried away that he had been a bit late going into his collected trot? Had they picked up on the split second he had hesitated when Charlotte had asked him for his half canter-pirouette?

Blueberry walked out of the arena, suddenly tired. The Prix St Georges tests were hard work but, as had become his habit after every test, the little brown horse lifted his head to look around at the people watching him. He always liked to show his appreciation for the crowds. Carl, as always, fell into step beside them as they made their way back to the horsebox, Lulu trotting alongside. Blueberry could hear Charlotte telling him that she wasn't happy with the test and that she could have done better. She didn't blame her mount, Blueberry acknowledged, but he knew it was a team effort and he wondered whether he could have listened more. Had he let himself get carried away? But it was so exciting competing at Prix St Georges, the movements were so uplifting!

"I blew it, Lulu," Blueberry said. "I was too keen; I should have listened to Charlotte more. I expect we've done badly. I've let everyone down."

"Stop that!" scolded Lulu. "Charlotte's grumbling about herself, not you. She, like all good riders, believes she could have ridden better and that the horse reflects the rider so stop blaming yourself. Gotta go," she added, turning back to Carl, who had been stopped by the interviewer from the television crew covering the Championships, and was being asked for his comments for viewers.

Lydia made Blueberry comfortable, telling him what a clever boy he was and how proud she was of him. Blueberry felt less cross with himself following Lulu's comments. He felt even better when the little dog appeared by his side a while later, breathless, having overheard Carl's interview with the television presenter.

"Big news, kiddo," she said, standing on three legs, a front paw up in the air, trembling with excitement from the tip of her nose to the end of her tail. "You'll never guess what it is!"

"Er…" Blueberry began, his mind whirling.

"Oh I can't wait," burst Lulu, "I've just seen your score and it's way better than anyone else's – even with those wobbles you think you had. You're the Prix St Georges National Champion. Congratulations!"

For once, Blueberry didn't know what to say. Could it really be true?

"That's not the best bit," continued Lulu, mysteriously.

"Nothing can be better than that," said Blueberry. He was so happy he felt as though

122

he might float upwards and drift across the showground like a big, brown, Blueberry balloon. The judges had liked his test. They had given him high scores. He and Charlotte were a brilliant team!

"Think again," said Lulu. "I've just heard Carl saying to the television camera – to camera mind, so there's no going back on it, or any chance he was joking – that he is training you and Charlotte with the next Olympic Games in mind. He says the Olympic Games due to be held at London in 2012 are his long-term goal for you both. What do you think of that?"

Blueberry didn't know what he thought of it, it was almost too big to take in. Could he and Charlotte really have a chance to compete at the next Olympic Games? Could it be possible?

"Uh-oh, here's Lydia with your tack," said Lulu. "It's time for the Prix St Georges prize-giving. But this is just the beginning of your international career, kiddo. If Carl's aim is true, then in two years' time you'll be competing at the Olympic Games in London. This kiddo, is where the real work begins!"

Coming soon…

Don't miss the next book in *The Blueberry Stories*, when Blueberry, Charlotte and Carl train hard to be selected for the London 2012 Olympic Games!

If you enjoyed reading this book you may want to answer these questions or discuss them with your friends or class at school:

Chapter I

1) After his training, Blueberry spends time in the solarium before returning to a full net of hay in his stable. What does that tell you about the care of horses at Brook Mill?

2) What does the expression *'…his appetite was legendary!'* mean?

Chapter 2

1) ' …*the leaves were thinking about turning to their autumn colours and drifting from the branches…*' What is the significance of the word *thinking*?

2) Blueberry's *'insecurities about his height'* are mentioned. Do you think these insecurities help or hinder Blueberry?

Chapter 3

1) Why didn't Lydia want to find Clyde in the Lane?

2) The word bonnet has two different meanings in chapter three. What are the two definitions?

Chapter 4

1) Blueberry and Orange have very different views on autumn. What do their views tell you about their individual characters too?
2) What is meant by the simile *'It's like trying to clip corrugated cardboard…'*

Chapter 5

1) What month is chapter five set in?
2) What do you imagine Blueberry is thinking as Emily pats his neck and tells him how well she thinks he's done?

Chapter 6

1) Why were the horses' buckets checked when the temperature dropped?
2) Do you imagine Blueberry would be as interested in television as Lulu is?

Chapter 7

1) If Carl was happy for his horses to stay at

Lucy's house for a couple of days, what facilities do you imagine it must have had?

2) Why do you think Lulu knows more about whether Carl would continue riding Blueberry than Blueberry himself?

Chapter 8

1) Do you think Lulu really did want to hear every detail of the Badminton Young Dressage Horse of the Future?

2) Thinking of all that Blueberry has learnt and had to consider in this chapter, what title might you give it?

Chapter 9

1) What does *'ebbed and flowed'* mean in the first sentence?

2) Why was a few days' experience at Brook Mill not something to be turned down?

Chapter 10

1) '… she always dropped by Blueberry's stable for a chat…' '… she offered him a tit-bit or two, stroking his forehead and talking gently to him.' What do these two quotations tell you about Roly as a 'half-sharer'?

2) Do you think Roly likes dogs? What helped you make your decision?

Chapter II

1) What does the analogy *'several forks in the road'* mean?
2) What is the literal translation of *'Grand Prix'*?

Chapter 12

1) What was it about Lulu that made Blueberry wish Lulu was at the Nationals with him?
2) *'All too soon the test was over...'* What does this tell you about Blueberry's attitude to the test?

Chapter 13

1) What do you think the old saying *'no foot, no horse'* actually means?
2) Do you think Blueberry may have understood Lulu's joke if he had seen the twinkle in Lulu's eye?

Chapter 14

1) Carl wished Blueberry's test was not one of the earliest. Knowing Orange's character, do

you think Carl would hope Orange's test to be early or late in the day?

2) Why is Lulu so sure that *'it's a mistake which won't happen again'*?

Chapter 15

1) Charlotte had whispered to Blueberry that she wanted him to have fun in the test. Do you think he did have fun?

2) Do you think Blueberry feels he has finally reached his dream of dancing like The Silver Dancer?

Blueberry Extras

Concentration

Blueberry is a horse who needs plenty of riding in, or warming up, before his tests. Each horse is different – some are ready after only a short warm up time but others, like Blueberry, are full of energy and need more work before they settle enough to compete to the best of their ability. Everyone thinks that practising the actual dressage test with the horse with which you are competing isn't a good idea because of the likelihood of the horse anticipating the movements, rather than listening for the rider's aids. This was never the case with Blueberry. I found that practising the test always worked for him. He knew what was coming, but never offered the movements before being asked. He really is an extraordinary horse!

When Blueberry and Charlotte lost the Advanced Medium Championship at the National Dressage Championships in 2009 it was only because of a moment's lost concentration. Something clattered in the walkway and because the test was early in the morning Blueberry had only been ridden in once, so he was still quite 'hot'. It just goes to show that there will always be something you haven't planned for – but maybe it was just as well it happened there, rather than in a more important competition later in Blueberry's career. You have to use hiccups like these to learn from – we didn't make that mistake again!

Breathe in... and out

How do you breathe when you are riding? It may sound like a strange question but breathing is something a lot of riders don't think about – and how they do it makes a difference to their riding. The next time you ride, be aware of how you inhale and expel a breath.

Some riders get breathless when riding: they concentrate so hard they forget to breathe, or they work so hard their breathing becomes laboured or tight. Good riders breathe regularly and rhythmically, giving their horse confidence and themselves plenty of air to work with.

If holding your breath is your problem, sing a tune as you ride to keep yourself breathing. Holding your breath can make some horses nervous; what are you worried about? Your horse will know what you're doing and he'll be worried, too. He'll think things must be bad if you're holding your breath!

If you run out of breath when you ride, make sure you are fit (riding when unfit is very unfair to yourself, not to mention your horse!), and that your horse or pony is schooled well enough to do the work you're asking of him, rather than making you do it all!

You can practise effective breathing without being on your horse or pony. Stand tall with good posture and put your hand on your chest, breathing in and out deeply. Does your chest go up and down? If so, you are breathing into your chest and this means you can only take a limited amount of air into your lungs. Also, as your chest moves, your upper body will move in the saddle, and your pony will feel that movement.

Now place your hand on your stomach and breathe in and out. If you are still breathing in your chest your hand won't move – but concentrate and take your breaths low until you do feel your hand moving as your diaphragm expands. Your chest should stay still. With practise, if you breathe like this on your horse or pony not only will you find you will be able to breathe more efficiently, but your lowered centre of gravity and still upper body helps your riding – and your horse!

The wanderer

Clyde the cat has become a wanderer, disappearing every now and again. We have come to accept that he may have another family he visits for weeks at a time, sharing his time between them and us, which was very worrying the first time until he returned to Brook Mill. That sort of thing happens with some cats, they do their own thing. Nobody really owns cats, do they? Their demeanour is such that they grace us with their presence, allow us to feed them, and tolerate our misplaced thoughts that they belong to us. I'm rather glad horses don't act the same way, I wouldn't be able to plan all the shows we go to if Blueberry disappeared to someone else's stable for weeks at a time!

Hair cut time!

The working horses at Brook Mill are all clipped through the winter. As explained in the book, this prevents them from sweating when they work hard, which could cause them to lose condition, or give them a chill as the sweat dries in the cold air. The coat grows again quite quickly so they are all clipped several times throughout the season. Each horse has a selection of rugs to wear, according to the temperature. Wearing a very thick rug on a mild day can cause a horse to overheat, just as his winter coat can make him sweat when he works, so we have lighter ones for the mild weather and bigger, thicker ones for when it gets really cold. Some horses have their legs bandaged at night when it's freezing. Most horses have their legs left unclipped, but dressage horses need to look slick, and besides, if they are washed off after work, fluffy legs would take ages to dry and stay cold in freezing weather, giving the horses freezing legs.

It's important not to let the horses get cold when we first bring them out for schooling and nobody dawdles, they mount quickly and get the horses moving. Taking their time is a good way to encourage the horses to find their own ways to get warm, and there is a danger of the riders having to deal with the odd buck! That's not a good idea – not only for the riders, but it wouldn't do for the horses to think bad manners were acceptable when they were working. In the school, it's serious work!

When hacking, we use three-quarter exercise sheets under the saddle and over the horses' quarters to keep their backs warm. The horses are allowed much more freedom out hacking and exuberant behaviour is accepted. They're not working, they're exercising, and it is important to make sure they understand the difference. The riders often have a hairy time out hacking when it's cold, or the wind blows up under the rugs. It keeps *them* on their toes!

The horses still go out in the field for some down-time all through the winter. They're rugged up with outdoor rugs and hoods, which cover their necks and – occasionally – their faces. This prevents mud from ruining their manes. The grooms don't enjoy peeling them off if the horses have rolled in the mud, they transfer all the sludge from the rugs (and hoods) to themselves!

Only the best will do

I am very careful to ensure that the people who care for our horses are at the top of their game. Our farrier at Brook Mill is a highly-respected expert on hoof health and care, and is consultant farrier to the British Equestrian Federation. Not only is he a brilliant farrier but the horses love him – and you can see he loves them back. You can get the occasional rough farrier, but it's not fair on the horses to be shouted at or treated less than respectfully so I would always advise care when finding one for your horse or pony. Blueberry never minds being shod and he lifts each leg up in turn to be treated. The dogs love our farriers, too, and they always form a canine audience who wait for the hoof trimmings to chew on. I don't understand it, they always smell disgusting – like cheesy feet – but you know what dogs are like. The smellier something is, the more they like it, take rolling in fox poo, for example!

Give something back

We have regular demonstrations at Brook Mill, sometimes held in conjunction with British Dressage. It gives people a chance to see behind the scenes at my dressage yard, ask questions and meet the horses – plus I enjoy being able to give something back. Everyone is always amazed at how ordinary life at Brook Mill is for the horses; they are all turned out (some live out in fields all year round), they're chilled when they are working and they love to interact with the visitors in the yard afterwards. And it's not just the horses who enjoy demos, the dogs love to practise their hosting skills, working the audience and choosing a lap or two to grace. It's great fun for everyone.

Time talk

The timescale for this book has been over several years – from 2006 to 2009 – and it may give the impression that working through the ranks in dressage is easy or quite quick. Of course, it isn't, and it takes a lot of time and effort to progress all the horses at Brook Mill through their career paths. I always have a lot of horses in training, at various stages, and each one deserves my full attention. Blueberry was always a clever horse, and his training went at quite a pace – but it can be tempting with a clever horse to push too hard, too soon.

It is vital to ensure a horse is not only in the right place in his training physically, but also mentally. He has to be able to process everything we ask from him so that he fully understands what he is being taught, is muscled up and physically fit enough to carry out the movements with ease, and progress with confidence, enjoying his work. Never rush your training. Always make sure your horse fully understands what you want him to do, and wait for your horse or pony to offer you more so that you know he is ready to go on to something more challenging. If, in your haste to succeed you rush, you run the risk of your horse or pony becoming confused, losing confidence and showing reluctance in his schooling. You want an enthusiastic partner, not one who dreads every session because he doesn't understand what you are asking him to do, or because you school for so long and so often that he has become bored and stale.

Above all, with everything you do with your horse or pony, make sure you both enjoy yourselves. It is a two-way thing, this riding, so make it as much about your mount as it is about yourself.

Glossary of equestrian terms introduced in book 3

Canter lead

The front (and hind) leg that leads and extends farthest is the leading leg in canter. It is considered correct for a horse or pony to lead with the inside leg when in an arena or cantering in a circle

Diagonal legs

At a trot or similar movement, the set of legs that move forward at the same time are the diagonal pair e.g. left foreleg and right hindleg

Overface

To ask a horse or pony during training or riding to do something that is beyond its capability or experience

Pirouette

A dressage movement performed in collected walk or canter where the horse or pony's front legs circle around the hind legs, with the inside hind leg stepping on almost the same spot. A full or 360-degree pirouette is expected to be six to eight steps and a half or 180-degree pirouette is expected to be three to five steps

Seat (Riders)

The seat is a combination of the rider's seat bones, pelvis and hips

Skipped out

To clear the horse droppings (manure) from a horse or pony's stable without fully mucking out or disturbing all the straw or shavings bedding

Solarium

A series of infra red lights fitted in a frame above horse height

Sound (term)

A sound horse or pony is one that has no lameness or illness

Stifle (or stifle joint)

The next joint above the hock in the hind leg of a horse or pony, the equivalent to a knee in humans

The Aids

An aid is the natural signal or means by which a rider asks a horse to do something by using his weight, legs, hands, seat, back, balance and voice

Transition

An upward or downward change of pace, from one pace to another e.g. walk to trot or within a pace e.g. working canter to medium or extended canter

Please see The Blueberry Stories books one and two for a glossary of terms introduced in earlier parts of the story